OTHER BOOKS BY THIS AUTHOR:

Out of the Storm

The Bridge Series

Deception Bridge
Broken Contracts

PREMONITION

Bridge

♣♥ GLORIA BOSTIC ♠♦

Year of the Book
135 Glen Avenue
Glen Rock, PA 17327

Print ISBN: 978-1-949150-23-0
eBook ISBN: 978-1-949150-33-9

Library of Congress Control Number: 2018958507

Scriptures taken from the Holy Bible, New International Version®, NIV®. Copyright © 1973, 1978, 1984, 2011 by Biblica, Inc.™ Used by permission of Zondervan. All rights reserved worldwide. www.zondervan.com The "NIV" and "New International Version" are trademarks registered in the United States Patent and Trademark Office by Biblica, Inc.™

DEDICATION

To Lee who is always by my side supporting me in all I do

To Mike, John, and Eddie who gave my life meaning

To my grandchildren who fill my life with joy

To my sister with whom I share my entire life's memories

Acknowledgments

There are so many to whom I am grateful for the completion of this, the final book of The Bridge Series. Always, of course, I am grateful to my family and friends for your love and support in all things, including my writing.

It began with the inspiration and support of a very special group of people sitting around the table in Glen Rock, Pennsylvania. These writers became my tribe, and they helped me find my way to acceptance of what I could accomplish by letting my thoughts pass through my fingertips onto the page.

Our tribe had a leader who became so much more. She is my editor who makes sure what I put on the page says and means what I intended. She puts it all together in a beautiful package with a cover designed from my chosen images but more elegant than I could have imagined. But above all that, she has become a friend I know I can always count on.

Thank you, Demi Stevens, for helping me learn to write with joy!

I must also acknowledge my readers. You give my words so much more meaning than I could give them alone, and the message you get from my words is uniquely yours. And knowing that is a great gift to me.

Finally, I thank God for all that I am and all that I am able to do.

Rescuer

Hope spoke quietly in my ear.
He took my hand and dried my tears...
with sword of truth He conquered strife
and chased despair from my life.
He slew the dragon I called Fright
and flooded me with His light.
Hope spoke quietly in my ear,
took my hand and dried my tears.

—G.K. Bostic

CHAPTER ONE – SUSAN

One year. *A moment and a lifetime ago.* Susan Walters stared at the coin in her hand. She stood at the bus stop waiting for her daughter, Elizabeth, and slipped the coin in her pocket at the sound of her name.

"Hi, Susan." It was one of her neighbors. One of the same neighbors who had snubbed her back in her drinking days. *But who could blame her?*

"Hi, looks like we're just in time," Susan said as the bus pulled up several minutes early. Susan was never late meeting Elizabeth these days. Funny how much things had changed since she'd turned her life around. After a year in recovery, it was still hard to think about what a mess she'd made of her life and how she could have lost her daughter forever. She did lose her husband... But maybe not forever.

Bounding off the bus, Elizabeth called, "Hi, Momma!" and raced her next-door neighbor and BFF, little Jordan, down the street to her driveway laughing all the way. This had become a daily ritual, and Elizabeth nearly always won. It was Jordan's mother, Amber, who had greeted Susan as the school bus approached, and now the two women shared a chuckle watching their first graders reach the finish line and then hug it out before each going to their own front door.

"Elizabeth has really shot up in the last few months, hasn't she?" Amber said. "Looks like she's at least a foot taller than Jordie now."

"Yeah, she's had quite a growth spurt," Susan agreed, "and it's no wonder. She has quite an appetite lately. Thank goodness she eats a lot of what's good for her. She loves her fruit." Susan grinned thinking about all the blueberries Elizabeth had eaten with her cereal that morning.

The short walk to their respective houses didn't allow time for an extended conversation, but before parting Amber mentioned something her daughter had told her the night before. "So Jordie says Elizabeth is all excited because her daddy's coming over to visit this weekend."

Susan saw the hopeful curiosity in the twinkle of her neighbor's eyes. With a sidelong glance she acknowledged the truth of it and wondered if Amber knew Elizabeth wasn't the only one excited about Marty coming over. *Of course, she knows. No sense trying to hide it.* "Yes, I planned one of his favorite meals, and Elizabeth is thrilled he's having dinner with us. Guess I'd better get cookin'. See you later."

"Okay. Have fun!" Amber called over her shoulder.

Susan could imagine the grin on her friend's face as she walked away. It was still hard for Susan to believe she and Amber had become such good friends in recent months. This was the same woman who had looked at her with utter disgust a little more than a year before. *But no wonder.* Susan could recognize it now. That woman—the woman Susan had been before her recovery— was disgusting. And she never wanted to be that person again.

"Hey Elizabeth, where'd you get to, kiddo?" Susan picked up the princess backpack carelessly tossed on the living room floor and carried it to her daughter's bedroom. "There you are. You forgot something, didn't you?"

"Oops," Elizabeth grinned up at her mother, "Sorry. Look, I'm making a picture for Daddy!"

Susan sat on the side of the bed and from her spot could watch as the child retrieved one crayon after another from the big jar on her little desk. "You're doing such a good job."

Elizabeth threw a huge toothless smile over her shoulder. "I'm going to be an artist like Mia when I grow up." She finished the masterpiece by printing 'I luv you Daddy' and chose the pink crayon to draw hearts all around the page.

"It's beautiful, sweetie. He'll love it." And she knew Marty would be delighted, as he always was by anything his little girl made for him. He had somehow overcome the knowledge she wasn't his biological child. She would always be his little girl. "Do you have any homework?" Susan asked.

"Oh, yeah," Elizabeth answered jumping up and pulling the large plastic bag out of her pack. She removed one of the little books and hopped onto the bed next to Susan. "Can I read it to you now?"

"You sure can. And maybe you can read it again when your daddy gets here."

Elizabeth gleefully agreed. Susan listened with delight as her daughter read the few words on each page then signed and dated the homework paper. She fleetingly gave thanks to the greater power allowing her to be present for her little girl.

"Okay, little one, how about a snack while Momma gets dinner started."

"Can I have some blueberries?"

"You're going to turn into a blueberry!" Elizabeth giggled as she followed her mother to the kitchen and opened the fridge. "How about a little glass of milk with that?"

Susan got her daughter settled at the island where they chatted while she fixed dinner—something she hadn't been able to do when Elizabeth was in kindergarten. Back then she had often been physically present but typically distracted, or worse, passed out.

***

"Lizzy!" Marty dropped to his knees just inside the front door, as Elizabeth ran into his arms. "Whoa! You're gettin' so big you almost knocked me over!" He squeezed his giggling little girl and winked over her shoulder at his ex. "And how's Momma?" he asked.

"I'm good." *Especially now that you're here.* "Do you want to show Daddy what you made for him?" Susan asked her daughter, securing his release.

He was duly thrilled with his little girl's gift and promised she would find it displayed on the refrigerator the next time she came to his house.

"I wish you could live here again so it could be on our fridge, and we could both see it every day."

"Come on, Elizabeth. We've talked about this..." Susan shrugged an apology at Marty and added, "Did you tell Daddy what we're having for dinner?"

"Mmmm, it smells awfully good." Marty hoisted his little Lizzy into his arms and headed for the kitchen. "Should I guess?"

"It's lasagna!" Elizabeth proclaimed before he had time to offer a guess.

"Smells delicious and I'm starving. Thank you, Suze."

Susan had fixed that particular dish because it was one of Marty's favorites, and his words warmed her and brought a memory from long ago—the day she'd prepared this very dinner to announce the good news of her pregnancy. The day she had decided this would be *his* child.

Marty had often called her Suze back then, but this was the first time she'd heard it since that dreadful day—the day she'd blurted out the truth and watched him walk out the door... *Let's not go there right now.*

Dinner was a great success, with Elizabeth, of course, being the entertaining center of attention. By the time they were digging into the Moose Tracks ice cream—also Marty's favorite—Elizabeth had exhausted her tales of first-grade antics and given her full attention to the large scoop of cold deliciousness before her. She pushed the tiny peanut butter cups to one side to save for last... just like Daddy did.

When she had stuffed the last bite into her mouth, she dropped the spoon in the bowl with a clang, sat back in her chair, and proclaimed, "I'm so full!"

Marty laughed, then scratched his head and said, "Hmm, I can't imagine why? I can't believe you didn't get a brain freeze as fast as you were shoveling that ice cream in."

Susan joined in the laughter but winced remembering the days she'd forgotten to prepare meals for her young child and how Elizabeth had crammed food in her mouth whenever it was there. But that was long ago. Surely her daughter knew she'd never go hungry again.

Marty helped clear the table then spent time with his little girl while Susan finished up in the kitchen. He listened as his Lizzy read her homework book then laughed and applauded in all the right places when she put on a show with her Kermit and Miss Piggy puppets.

Susan peeked in on them a little later, and discovered her daughter was in her PJs, propped up against the pillows, listening raptly to Marty reading *If You Give a Mouse a Cookie.*

She stood in the doorway, loving the scene before her, wishing it could be like that every night—the way it had been before she ruined everything. *This is where you belong, Marty.*

As if he'd read her mind—or at least sensed her presence—Marty looked up. "This is nice." He spoke softly, ruffling his child's curly red hair. "Thanks for suggesting it, Suze." There it was again, his pet name for her. Elizabeth rubbed her eyes and yawned. "I think somebody's sleepy," he added.

Susan glanced at her watch. "I think Daddy's right, Elizabeth. It's past your bedtime. Time for hugs and kisses, then off to dreamland."

"I don't want to go to dreamland." The smile on the child's face faded, her eyes widened and her chin quivered.

"Why is that, Lizzy?" Marty brushed the red curls from her forehead.

"I don't like my dreams. They're scary. Last night I dreamed about an ugly man. He was bad." Elizabeth was on the brink of tears.

Susan moved closer and sat at the foot of the bed. "What do you mean, kiddo? What did he do?"

"I don't know. He just looked mean and scary. I didn't like his whiskers, and I don't think that girl wanted to go with him." After a little reassurance and lots of hugs and kisses, Elizabeth yawned again and slid down on her pillows. She was finally ready to say goodnight. There had been no further details of the unsettling dream.

Back in the living room, Susan and Marty settled on the sofa like the two good friends they'd become again over the past year. But tonight felt different to Susan. Especially when he reached over and took her hand.

Chapter Two – Sarah

Waiting at the red light, Sarah's eyes were drawn toward the metallic blue Chevy pickup that pulled up on her left. She met the dark stare of a young man with straggly brown hair and an unkempt moustache. He looked vaguely familiar. Her head snapped forward as the light turned green, and she crossed the intersection relieved the Chevy turned left onto Route 30. *"That wasn't him!"* She tried to shake off the remnants of what her last client had revealed.

Steering with her right, Sarah Reed pulled her other hand off the wheel, rubbed the gooseflesh on her arm, and let out a low whistle. *Get a grip. You're imagining things.*

Sarah pulled into the convenience store parking lot, parked, and went inside. She made a quick withdrawal at the ATM and grabbed a Frappuccino and candy bar—not that she needed it, but she always felt compelled to make a purchase once in the store. Back in her car, Sarah's gaze darted around for any sign of the pickup, before she chastised herself. *Now you're just being paranoid.*

Putting aside the memory of her last client's warnings and the resulting disquiet, Sarah focused on all she needed to get done in the next few hours. It was bridge night, but at least it was at Val's and not her house, so she didn't have to worry about picking up after the kids. Still, the next few hours would be full and busy.

When she got home, Sarah was greeted by the aroma of tater-top sloppy joes wafting from the crock-pot and the peaceful quiet of being the first one home. Sarah loved her big family but also enjoyed the luxury of these quiet intervals. Relieved she didn't have to prepare dinner, Sarah glanced at the time, stepped out of her shoes, and headed for the master bedroom in the back of the house and a quick shower. Craig always picked up Destiny from the babysitter on Tuesdays and Thursdays and the kids didn't get off the bus 'til almost four o'clock, so it would be nearly an hour before the house would come alive.

Sarah breathed in the steam and sweet scent of her shampoo and let the hot water wash the day's stress down the drain. It wasn't until she stepped out of the shower and heard a noise that Holly's warning came rushing back to her.

"Sarah, you should have heard him. He sounded crazy. I mean he wasn't rational."

Sarah hadn't seen her old client since she discharged Holly over a year earlier. So, when Holly called declaring she needed to talk to her right away, Sarah had immediately made room in her busy schedule.

Now her client's words echoed in her mind. *"He kept screaming it was all your fault, Sarah. He said you messed me up, and we were fine before I started therapy and let you interfere in our lives. I tried to tell him I never would have come to therapy if it weren't for the abuse, but he wouldn't listen. He won't admit he did anything wrong, and he can't tolerate not getting his way."*

As a therapist, Sarah knew empowering her clients so they were strong enough to get out of abusive relationships would always anger the abusers, but Holly was convinced her ex might now be dangerous.

Her final words rang in Sarah's brain. *"He said 'I'll make her pay!' Sarah, and he said he'd get even. I think he's off his meds, and I'm afraid of what he might do."*

Sarah wrapped the towel tightly around her torso and put her ear against the condensation-streaked bathroom door. Nothing. The only sound, the shower dripping on wet tile. Her breath came in short pants, pulse throbbing in her throat. If only she could get dressed before opening that door, but with no one home, she hadn't seen a need to bring her clothes into the bathroom with her or hang her robe on the hook. Now she felt utterly exposed and vulnerable.

Screwing up her courage—all the while thinking how stupid she thought women in movies were for doing it—she reached for the doorknob.

Thump... Sarah jerked back her hand. All doubt disappeared. Sarah sucked in her breath... *There's someone in the bedroom.* Frantically looking around the bathroom for some kind of weapon to defend herself, she grabbed her hairdryer.

"Hey angel, I'm home."

Craig's voice forced the air out of her as she dropped the hairdryer, threw open the door and ran into his arms.

"Wow, that's a better greeting than I expected." Sarah heard the laughter in his voice as tears of relief rushed down her cheeks. "Whoa, what's wrong?" He pushed her an arm's length away and looked into her tear-filled eyes. "You're shaking... hey," he pulled her close again, "I'm here. It's okay. Whatever it is... breathe, angel. Tell me..."

Sarah slowed her gasps, and when she could speak, asked, "What, wh-what are you doing here? I mean, you're early. I didn't expect you 'til after four o'clock."

"Yeah, but we got lucky. Jack had to attend a principal's conference so he cancelled the faculty meeting. I thought I'd surprise you, not scare you to death," he added. "Seriously, is that it? Did I startle you? Seems like something more..."

Sarah saw the concern in his eyes, but decided there was no need to alarm him. After all, she was being ridiculous. "I, I just didn't expect you," she laughed then added, "and I envisioned that scene from *Psycho.*" Even as she tried to make light of her fear, she couldn't stop shaking.

"You're shivering," Craig said rubbing her arms.

"Yeah, I'd better get dressed before I freeze." Sarah wrapped the towel tighter and wiped the water dripping down her neck.

"Whoa, not so fast. I've got a better idea how to warm you up." Craig slid the towel to the floor and wrapped her in his arms.

"But what about the baby?" Sarah murmured. "Is she sleeping?"

"I didn't pick her up yet. They don't expect me for another forty-five minutes."

Sarah saw the devil in his eyes, and being familiar with that look, her heart jumped in anticipation. Craig slowly backed her toward the bed, then swooped her up and gently deposited her onto the four-poster. Watching in admiration as he quickly removed his clothes, she forgot all about the need to dry her hair. His body was as firm and muscular as the first time she'd seen him like this. He was ready... and now—with all thoughts of her earlier scare dismissed—so was she.

CHAPTER THREE – VAL

Val paused in her preparations to gaze out the kitchen window and breathe in the freshness of spring. The fragrance of newly mown grass was like an elixir to her winter woes. Too long confined indoors, she delighted in throwing open the windows. The early evening chill would soon force her to close every sash, but she chose to savor a few more moments before doing so.

"Okay sweetheart, I'm heading over to the kids' house. Can I help you with anything else before I go?" Andy would spend the evening with their son and five grandchildren—as was his habit when Val hosted card club—while the women gathered for their weekly bridge game. He said he left to "get out of the ladies' hair," but everyone knew he loved nothing more than spending time with Craig and the kids.

"Yes, could you close the other windows before you go, please?" She grudgingly shut and latched the one over the sink. "Oh, and thanks for mowing. It was really getting high with all the rain this week."

"Already got most of them," he said heading back to finish the task. "I just thought I'd do the downstairs last..." he called over his shoulder. "I figured you'd want to get lots of fresh air in the house before you ladies filled it with hot air."

Val joined his laughter, granting there would soon be a lot of chatter 'round the card table. That was, after all, the best part of their gatherings.

Andy stopped for a quick kiss and a long embrace before leaving. The passing years, with all their trials and tribulations, had taught them the importance of staying close and holding on. Those hugs said 'I love you' and so much more. They were an even stronger elixir than the fresh spring air.

"Make sure you give big hugs all around from Grandma, and extra baby snuggles to the little one." Destiny had been a special addition to Sarah and Craig's blended family. With Craig's children, Mia and Cody, and Sarah's kids, Julie and Bobby, Destiny made five.

There had been some concern there might be jealousy with a new baby in the house, but the other children seemed to adore her. Bobby, being the youngest, had been their greatest concern—and he had taken the longest to warm up to the new baby of the family—but given certain responsibilities, Bobby now considered his role as big brother one of honor and importance. Of course, most of the credit had to go to Sarah. She made sure her youngest son felt the full measure of her love even when baby Destiny was in her arms... even when she felt the utter exhaustion only the mother of a newborn understands.

"Hello?"

"Hi Bonnie... in the kitchen," Val called out to her best friend. With her open-door policy, the bridge ladies didn't bother to knock on Thursday nights. "You're the first one here."

Val's daughter-in-law, Sarah, and the youngest player in the group, Kathy, arrived moments later and gathered around the table with snacks, cards, and lots of friendly chatter.

"I think she'll be taking her first steps any day now," Sarah told them. The baby's progress and antics in general were always one of the first topics of conversation, and as Destiny grew, the ladies all looked forward to hearing the latest. "She's crawling all over the place, and Bobby's starting to realize he can't leave anything within her reach. He even warns his brother and sisters to pick up their things."

This got a chuckle from everyone since they'd often heard how Sarah struggled to get Bobby to pick up after himself. His grandma had witnessed this first-hand.

"Well, how about that? It took Destiny to teach my grandson to be tidy," Val said.

"Oh, I wouldn't go that far, Mom," Sarah said. "Dessie can't get in Bobby's bedroom, and if you open the door to that mess, you wouldn't exactly call him tidy. The one whose room is always neat and spotless is Julie's, and I swear she didn't get that gene from me."

"Tell them the latest news about Mia," Val urged.

"Oh, is it about the art show?" Bonnie asked.

"Yes! She got first place!" Val exclaimed. "Oh, sorry Sarah." She winked. "I didn't mean to jump in and steal your thunder."

"No worries, a proud grandma has a right to share." Sarah picked up the cards she'd been dealt and while she arranged the suits, added, "And I think it's justified. The art teacher told me Mia's work is exceptional and holds real promise. She said it has kind of a mystical flavor that makes people feel something."

Bonnie nodded. "I would agree. I've felt it."

Val and Sarah smiled knowingly.

Kathy alone looked confused. "I'm not sure what that means, but I'd love to see more of her art. I know from your phone shots she does amazing pieces for a twelve year old, or any age for that matter."

But Val and Sarah exchanged glances. They shared a knowledge that some of Mia's drawings were haunting—perhaps even frightening.

The cards, bidding, and conversation continued round the table as Bonnie and Val won the first rubber and Sarah and Kathy took the second. "Does anyone need refills before we start the tie-breaker?" Val asked.

In the kitchen Val took the opportunity to check in with Kathy. "You haven't had a lot to say tonight. How are you doing?" It had been nearly two months since Kathy discovered her husband had cheated on her with more than one other woman, and she had been devastated.

"I'm okay," Kathy answered, "or at least I will be. And to think, I wanted to have his children."

GLORIA BOSTIC

Val rushed to embrace her young friend when she saw those eyes glistening with unshed tears, but after several seconds, Kathy pulled back, took a deep breath, and grinned. "Seriously Val, I'm going to be fine. Better to find out now than after having a child." And Val knew that was true.

She also knew not many marriages could survive infidelity. She and Andy were a rare exception, and it was only faith, forgiveness, and having God at the center of their relationship that had pulled them through.

Back at the table—as though Bonnie had read her mind—she asked, "Val, how's Betsy doing?"

Betsy was the product of her husband, Andy's, indiscretion nearly eight years ago. The seven-year-old girl had even spent several months as their foster child when her mother had been incarcerated for wrecking the car while intoxicated—and with Betsy in the backseat.

"She's doing really well from what I've heard. Sarah, have you seen her lately?"

"Yes, she still loves to come over and watch movies with the kids. And Mia loves having her there. I'm pretty sure Susan's dropping her off this evening while she goes to her Thursday night meeting." Betsy's mother, Susan, attended her AA meetings faithfully, and they had all seen her transforming back into the beautiful, healthy woman she'd been before her addiction nearly destroyed her.

Eventually Val had managed to forgive the woman who slept with her husband, but resentment tiptoed into her thoughts when she imagined Andy with Susan's daughter—his daughter—the child of his infidelity.

Chapter Four – Bonnie

After a nearly five-minute animated greeting and a brisk fifteen-minute walk, Bonnie gave Ginger her treat and settled into her favorite recliner. She patted her lap, and the little Pomeranian instantly responded by joining her.

"Are you comfy, Gingersnap?" She scratched her tiny companion behind the ears, accepted a few excited kisses, and giving her a little hug, laughed at the dog's antics. "I don't know what I'd do without you, girl."

Bonnie had gotten Ginger to help fill the emptiness after she lost Frank, her husband of many years. In the months following his death, the quiet stillness of her home became unbearable. Ginger was the cure. Her warm greetings and constant companionship eased the loneliness and made life more bearable.

Absently turning the ringer back on and checking her phone, Bonnie saw a missed call from Joe. More recently, he had also helped fill the void. A widower himself, and an old friend of hers and Frank's, Joe Marconi understood what she was going through better than anyone else in her close circle of friends.

She hesitated, debating whether to return his call before going to bed or to wait until morning. After all, Joe knew she always turned her phone off on bridge night. "Should I call him, Ginger? It's getting late, but it would be nice to hear his voice before we hit the hay, huh?"

As soon as the words fell out of her mouth, an old familiar niggling guilt crept in behind them. She quickly pushed it aside and hit *call back*. Joe answered after one ring.

"So, who were the big winners tonight? Or is that a silly question?" Joe asked.

Bonnie heard the laughter behind his words and could envision the light in his eyes. She liked the warmth of his smile and the twinkle in his big brown eyes. And unlike so many men his age, he still had a thick, full head of hair combed straight back in the fashion of Michael Corleone in *The Godfather*. But he was the antithesis of such a character. Joe was a kind and gentle man. In that way he was very much like her husband, Frank, had been. Bonnie could never imagine being with any other kind of man.

The two friends chatted comfortably until Bonnie caught herself stifling a yawn and checked the time. "My goodness, Joe, do you realize we've been talking for more than half an hour?"

"I'm sorry, my dear. I didn't intend to keep you so long."

"No, don't be silly. You know I enjoy our talks, but I think I'd better go over my Bible study notes before I get too sleepy. It wouldn't do for the group leader not to be familiar with the day's topic."

"It's hard to imagine there's any part of the Bible with which you're not familiar, my dear, but I'll let you go."

Again, Bonnie heard the laughter behind Joe's teasing... and it made her smile. "Thanks, Joe. Talk to you tomorrow." After putting the phone on its charger, she opened the armoire and slowly read the words for the next morning's Bible study.

Ecclesiastes 3:1-8: *"There is a time for everything, and a season for every activity under heaven: a time to be born and a time to die, a time to plant and a time to uproot, a time to kill and a time to heal, a time to tear down and a time to build, a time to weep and a time to laugh, a time to mourn and a time to dance, a time to scatter stones and a time to gather them, a time to embrace and a time to refrain, a time to search and a time to give up, a time to keep and a time to throw away, a time to tear and a time to mend, a time to be silent and a time to speak, a time to love and a time to hate, a time for war and a time for peace."*

She leaned back reflecting in the stillness of the late hour. Ginger was taking her pre-bedtime nap. There was no sound of TV or music playing. All Bonnie heard was the ticking clock on the wall and the words reverberating in her mind. She knew the passage by heart, of course, but tonight the words penetrated deep into her soul. Not all the words. Just the ones God seemed to be whispering to her.

... a time to weep and a time to laugh, a time to mourn and a time to dance.

... a time to weep and a time to laugh, a time to mourn and a time to dance.

The words kept repeating until she finally whispered back. "But Lord, how do I know which it is? When is it time to stop mourning? How do I know?"

Ginger stirred, shook, then bounded over to Bonnie, bringing her back to the need of the moment. Her furrowed brow relaxed as she cradled her little furball. "Yes, Ginger, you're right. It's time for us to get ready for bed. Ah, a time to wonder and worry... and a time to sleep." But much later, having read her devotions and said her prayers, Bonnie's thoughts returned to the question... *Is it time—could it be—time to dance?*

CHAPTER FIVE – VAL

As they sang the opening hymn, Val noticed her best friend looking at something or someone toward the back of the church. From her vantage point in the choir loft, Bonnie could apparently see something of enormous interest, and Val's curiosity was piqued. She wriggled in her seat until she could no longer resist the urge to discover what was putting that sweet smile of satisfaction on her friend's face.

As discreetly as possible, she glanced over her right shoulder and followed Bonnie's gaze until her eyes fell on the three people she realized Bonnie was watching. Susan Walters looked almost as young and attractive as she had years ago before alcohol had stolen her beauty. Now, no longer so painfully skinny with cheeks sunken in, her blonde hair carefully coiffed, and face fairly glowing, she looked like the old Susan.

But Susan's appearance wasn't that surprising since Val had run into her occasionally. The real surprise was seeing Marty seated to her left. And there—between them—sat Betsy. The adorable child, with her red curls, had asked Val and Andy to call her Betsy when they fostered her, and little Elizabeth would forever be Betsy in her eyes. *She certainly looks like she could be Marty's child.* Marty used to have his own red hair cropped short, but was wearing it longer these days. The deep rich auburn color— the color that had assured them all Betsy surely must be his child— still helped make it believable.

As Val turned back to face the front of the church, Andy took her hand in his, and she realized he had also seen the little family behind them. She looked up into eyes that spoke volumes. That was all the reassurance she would ever need. Val's lips curled upward, and she gave her husband's hand an answering squeeze.

Singing the final 'Amen' she looked toward the choir loft and made eye contact with Bonnie who she now realized had been watching her. Val recognized that look. It also said 'Amen.'

As the service proceeded, Val didn't think any more about the Walters until Pastor Barns began his sermon. She wondered at his uncanny habit of preaching about exactly what was most relevant in her life in that moment. Today his sermon was on starting over.

"I would venture there is not one among us who has not made a mistake. Not one among us who has made a decision we didn't regret. Not one among us who hasn't wanted to go back and undo some part of our past. But we can't! No, we can't go back and undo our past mistakes... But... with Jesus we can start over."

Val knew this was true. She and Andy had started over, but it was only with God at the center of their lives that it had been possible. Now, listening to Pastor Barns, she thought of Susan and Marty and wondered if they too could start over. It certainly couldn't be easy for Marty, but over the past year Val believed he and Susan had been slowly reconnecting. Maybe, just maybe...

***

"Do you believe in miracles?" Andy asked as they slowly sidled out of their pew following the benediction.

Val knew what he meant immediately. "Yes, I do, and I believe we may be witnessing one," Val whispered.

"Elizabeth!" Val heard Susan's soft call to her daughter just before she was nearly knocked down by the little one's hug.

"Hi, Aunt Val. Did you know I was in grownup church today? Daddy came with us, and I didn't go to children's chapel. I got to sit with him and Momma."

"I'm sorry, Val," Susan apologized. "She got away from me before I realized what was happening."

"No worries. We're always happy to see this little sweetie."

Before she could say more Betsy jumped in. "Where's Mia?"

"She and Julie and the boys all went to Children's Chapel. Aunt Sarah and Uncle Craig went to get them. They'll be out on the parking lot shortly if you want to see them." Val glanced at Susan, wondering if she'd overstepped but was relieved to see her nod in agreement.

"Yay, Momma, can we?" Getting her mother's permission, she turned to Marty. "C'mon, Daddy. Let's go see Mia."

"I guess Lizzy and I are heading outside." Marty winked over his shoulder as the child tugged him forward.

Susan watched the two heading through the narthex but lingered behind and turned to Val and Andy. "She really loves her Daddy. I mean..." Susan looked down at the floor, and Val saw the color rising in her cheeks.

Val rushed to put her at ease. "Of course she does! And anyone can see Marty feels the same about her."

"Absolutely!" It was the first word Andy had uttered since the encounter, and Val appreciated his effort to also put Susan at ease. She could see the same appreciation in the other woman's eyes. By the time they made their way outside to the parking lot, a little reunion was taking place by Craig's van.

Val shaded her eyes from the sun. "Look at them, Andy." Susan had hurried ahead to catch up with her Elizabeth, and Val was happy to take her time getting there. "I'm always amazed by the bond between those two," she said, watching Mia and Betsy.

During the months Susan had been serving her sentence for driving under the influence and child endangerment, and after she was released and getting sober, her little girl had lived with them—never knowing Andy was her biological father—and grown quite attached to Andy and Val's grandchildren. Especially Mia.

Although Craig and Sarah had finally been told the secret, none of the grandchildren had any idea Betsy was actually Craig's sister and their aunt.

Nevertheless, the kids had formed such a close attachment Val, Andy, and Susan agreed to allow the friendship to continue. Though a bit awkward at first, with Andy being most concerned about his wife, Val convinced him she was okay with it. After all, she had come to love Betsy, and most of the 'play dates' took place at Craig and Sarah's, often while Susan attended her AA meetings.

"Andy..." Val had stopped before reaching the small group congregating around the white Dodge Caravan and put her hand on her husband's arm.

"Hmm?"

"Look at them. It's like they belong together."

"I think you're right, and maybe, just maybe, Marty has forgiven her, and they can get past all that's happened. Susan certainly isn't the same train wreck she was when she was drinking."

"No, I'm not talking about them," Val interrupted. "I mean, yeah, you might be right about them—I hope so—but I meant Mia and Betsy. Every time I see them together, it amazes me."

Andy nodded in agreement. "Yeah, they've made quite a connection."

But Val had a feeling she couldn't really put into words. She had watched them play together. She had watched them pray together. And at this moment, standing there chatting and giggling, they appeared to be encased in a sunbeam. And even at this distance, standing in the shade of the church, Val could feel the warmth.

CHAPTER SIX – SARAH

Sarah's head snapped up, and her hand trembled. Mia's drawing slipped from her fingers.

"What's wrong, Mom? Don't you like it?" Mia's face crumbled as she spoke, and Sarah hurried to compose herself.

"No, Mia, don't be silly. It's so good. I love all your drawings. You know that."

"But, but you chucked it. And you made a face."

Sarah stooped to pick Mia's art project off the desk where it had landed. "No honey, really, I just dropped it when I remembered I've gotta get those potatoes peeled or your grandparents will be here, and I won't have dinner ready." She looked at the image before her and forced a smile. "Actually, I think this may be one of your best. Where is this?"

"Nowhere. I mean it's just a pretty place I imagined. Do you really like it?"

"Definitely." Sarah pulled the young artist close and kissed the top of her head. "Honestly, I think your work is inspired." She handed the drawing back to Mia and added, "You'll have to show it to Grandma when she gets here... which is going to be pretty soon. Wanna help me in the kitchen?"

"Sure. Hey, Julie!" Mia shouted down the hall. "Come help get dinner!"

Before long, Julie and Mia were setting the table while Sarah put the pot of potatoes on to boil. She jumped when Craig quietly came up behind her and put his arms around her waist, then slumped against him.

He kissed her neck before asking, "Can I help?"

"Mmm, you already have." Sarah turned in her husband's arms and enjoyed the feel of his lips on hers. But not for long.

"Ew, yuck, they're kissing again!" It was Bobby who then made kissy noises. Cody joined in until Craig turned and went on the chase. Sarah heard them fall into a jumble of giggles and could picture them toppling onto the big, comfy sectional in the family room.

Sarah leaned against the sink staring out over the lovely spring scene, but all she really saw was Mia's picture. Another serene setting with lush greens, and a little bridge leading to an enchanting cabin in the woods. It was hauntingly beautiful. *But why does it make my blood run cold?* Her thoughts were interrupted by the sound of Destiny waking from a nap followed by the cacophony of shouting and laughing that indicated Grandma and Grandpa had arrived.

When the roast and all the side dishes were brought in, everyone gathered around the long dining table and joined hands for grace. Sarah listened as Mia—whose turn it was to say the blessing—gave thanks for all her family, the food they were about to receive, and a final thank you for the individual gifts and talents He had given each of them.

Sarah understood that Mia now grasped the extent of her own artistic ability and what a gift she'd been given... especially when she created her inspired drawings and paintings. Those were the ones Mia explained she didn't plan.

The images came into her head, and she felt compelled to get them on paper. These pictures often evoked emotional responses from those who viewed them. Some were simply beautiful, picturesque, almost spiritual. Some were more haunting, and to Sarah, frightening. She thought of the picture she'd held before dinner.

"Everything looks and smells delicious," Val said.

"I think she means let's eat." Craig grinned at his wife as he passed the roast to Andy, sitting at his right. "Dig in, Dad."

Before long, plates were piled high, and the usual Sunday dinner conversation—primarily dominated by the kids—ensued with youthful fervor.

Even Destiny added her two cents with gurgles and coos as her momma shoveled in the mashed potatoes, trying to keep up with the child's hardy appetite. When the baby finished those and began working on her teething cookie, Sarah tuned back in on the dinner conversation.

"*A Wrinkle in Time*? Haven't you read that before?" Val asked Julie.

"Yeah, twice." Julie's eyes crinkled. "I love it."

Val nodded. "I get that. There aren't many books I'd read more than once, but there've been a few. When I was your age, I think I read *Little Women* at least three times." Turning to Mia, she asked, "So what about you? Any new creations I haven't seen?"

"A couple."

"Oh Mia, how about the one you showed me before dinner?" Sarah chimed in. "You've gotta show that to Grandma after dessert." And as soon as the child put her fork down after the last bite of cobbler, Sarah blurted, "Mia, you may be excused if you want to go get your picture." Catching the quizzical glance from Val, Sarah added, "I think it's one of the special ones."

That got Craig's attention as well, and when Mia returned with the drawing, Sarah watched as her husband and in-laws passed it back and forth praising her skill.

"Beautiful, Mia." Craig nodded and smiled, but Sarah saw no alarm in his reaction to the image.

Of course not. Why would he see it? Sarah wiped the baby's face and took Destiny out of the highchair.

"Look at the detail," Val said. "I like how you show there's someone at the cabin by adding the pickup truck."

Sarah froze.

Forcing herself to move again, Sarah signaled the end of dinner. "Okay kids, clear the table, please." She turned to face her in-laws. "I'm gonna go change this little one, and I think she's about ready for her afternoon nap. It's so gorgeous out today, why don't you all take your coffee out on the deck, and I'll join you as soon as I get Destiny settled?"

"I've got an even better idea," Val said reaching for her youngest grandchild. "How 'bout if Grandma takes this precious little one, and you go relax? That's a win-win, okay?"

When Val finally joined them on the deck, Cody and Bobby were down in the grass beyond the pool tossing a football with their dad and grandpa. "Football in May?" she asked.

"Yep, they never seem to get tired of that, especially when they can talk Craig and Andy into joining them. And I'm glad to see them outdoors again." Even though they had rules about how much time they could use them, Sarah worried the boys spent too much time playing video games and hanging indoors.

"And where are the girls?" Val asked.

"They took Goldie for a walk. Julie was heading to her room to read, but Mia talked her into going along. They love that dog!"

The rest of Sarah's bridge group had questioned her sanity when she told them about the Golden Retriever puppy they were getting while expecting a new baby, but they'd been wrong. Goldie was a great addition to their family, and all the kids adored her... especially Destiny.

"So, everyone ran off and deserted you, huh?"

Sarah chuckled. "I'm not complaining. An occasional serene respite isn't a problem." She breathed in the sweet smell of spring and exhaled slowly, releasing the last bit of tension from her shoulders. But her serenity was interrupted by Val's next words.

"So, Sarah, tell me. What's your reaction to Mia's drawing all about?"

Sarah glanced at Val who sipped her coffee and looked over the rim of her mug with interest.

"Oh, nothing specific really," Sarah lied. "It's just... I don't know. I do wonder sometimes where some of these images come from." She wasn't ready to share her concerns with her mother-in-law. Besides, she was certain she was being ridiculous.

It doesn't mean anything. Sarah kept telling herself it didn't mean anything, but she wasn't convinced. After all, adding the detail of a truck to her picture was no big deal. *But why did it have to be a metallic blue Chevy pickup?*

Chapter Seven – Val

Val studied her daughter-in-law's profile as she absently swirled the last bit of coffee in her cup. She considered pursuing the question of Sarah's apparent concern about Mia's drawing… because there was obviously more going on with her than she was letting on.

But as she opened her mouth to speak, Sarah turned to her with laughter in her eyes. "Well, Val, there goes the serenity!"

Mia, Julie, and Goldie had rounded the corner of the house and sprinted toward them. With the girls giggling and the dog panting, the three collapsed onto the deck and launched into an account of their encounter with old Mr. Sam and Ellie, his German Shepherd.

"You should've seen it," Julie said, still out of breath. "Goldie got so excited, and she wanted to play. She kept running up to Ellie and then she'd put her front paws down—you know like she does when she wants you to chase her—and…"

"Yeah," Mia chimed in, "and Ellie thinks she's crazy. She just yawned and then laid right down."

"And Mr. Sam said 'the old gal can't keep up with your young'un' and he laughed." Mia and Julie had met Sam Lathom soon after moving into their new home, and they immediately fell in love with him and his gorgeous German Shepherd. At thirteen years of age, though, Ellie moved a little slower than their Goldie who still had her puppy playfulness.

"And I think you've worn this young'un out," Sarah said looking at the dog's tongue hanging out the side of her mouth. "You ought to take her in and give her fresh water."

"Okay, Mom. C'mon, Mia! C'mon, Goldie!" Julie called. And with that, the whirlwind swept through the French doors and left the deck in peaceful tranquility once more.

"More coffee, Val?"

"No, I'm good. But do you want me to get you another cup?" Val figured Sarah might need the caffeine to keep up with her busy family, but she declined the offer.

Sarah checked the time on her Fitbit, and glanced at the baby monitor on the side table. "I'm surprised Dessi is sleeping this long." And as if on cue, they heard the first coos. Destiny usually woke from her afternoon nap in a pleasant mood and was often content to lie there for a while before insisting it was time to get up.

But Val wasn't so content to leave her there. "Can I go get her?" She knew Sarah wouldn't mind at all, and she cherished those moments of caring for her youngest grandchild.

Her heart swelled when the baby greeted her with a big smile of recognition and anticipation. As she lifted Destiny from the crib, she breathed in the sweet scent of her hair. The little one was still sleepy enough to calmly rest her head on Val's shoulder, and Grandma soaked in the moment... until a new scent assaulted her nose.

"Whoa," Val said, heading for the changing table. "You are so stinky-poo!"

"Here let me take care of that." Sarah had quietly entered the room, but Val laughed.

"No, I've got this," she told Sarah. "Are the boys still playing ball?"

"No, Cody and Bobby wore the old guys out. Would you believe, after that big dinner, they all came in and asked for snacks?"

Val had no trouble believing it. She was familiar with their hardy appetites.

"How about you, Val? Would you like something? I made brownies."

"That's tempting, but no. I'm going to have to shop for a size bigger if you keep trying to fatten me up, girl." Handing Destiny over to her mother—the baby was reaching for her favorite person in the world—Val asked, "Cobbler and brownies? You've been busy."

"Yeah, well, Susan is going to be dropping Betsy off later while she goes to her AA meeting, and you know Betsy loves her brownies."

"Oh, what time is she coming over?" Val had mixed feelings of anticipation and dread.

"Probably about five or five-fifteen. Susan's meeting is at six. Do you want to stick around and see her?"

Val knew she meant Betsy, not Susan, but unless the first-grader was driving herself over, they were kind of a package deal.

"No, I think we're going to be heading home shortly. I still want to finish my article today, and I think Andy might do some yard work." Since Val had started doing freelance work, she had to be mindful of deadlines. And that was as good a reason as any to hit the road before Susan arrived.

Back in the family room, Val maneuvered her way to a spot next to Andy on the sectional and looked around at the homey scene. Destiny jumped and moved about in her walker while Bobby entertained her with his silly antics. The adults, all seated on the sectional, seemed engrossed in watching them as well as Cody, Mia, and Julie's game of Uno.

"Wow, look at the time," Val said checking her watch. "Where did the afternoon go? Are you about ready to hit the road, hon?" she asked Andy.

"Yeah, it is almost five o'clock already, and the boys about wore me out," her husband answered.

"Aw, do you have to go?" Bobby asked.

"Can't you stay and play one game of Uno with us?" Cody pleaded.

Val resisted the temptation. "No, not today. Grandma has writing to do, and you know that game can go on and on sometimes."

Andy agreed, and they stood to leave, but Mia asked them to wait as she dashed out of the room.

She returned with the drawing in her hands and ran over to Val. "This is for you," she said handing the paper to her grandma who was both pleased and surprised. Mia had often made drawings for Val to put on the fridge when she was younger but rarely did so these days.

"Thank you, Mia," Val said. "I love it. I think I'd like to frame this one and hang it on the wall in my office. What do you think?"

Mia nodded enthusiastically, face glowing, but Val noticed a distinctly different expression on her mother's face. Though Sarah recovered quickly, Val hadn't missed the sudden furrowing of her brows. "Unless your Momma would like to keep it here?"

Mia's eyes widened and her head swung to look at Sarah.

"No, don't be silly," Sarah said. "Of course, your grandma can have it. I'll take the next one, okay?" Her wink seemed to reassure Mia who hugged her grandma extra tight before she left.

***

Back at home, Val was true to her word and settled in with a glass of Chardonnay and her laptop. She reread her travel article—what she had so far—and found it easy to do the final closing summary. The people she'd met in Savannah were generous with their knowledge of the area and its history and shared several amusing anecdotes that gave it just the right punch. *That's good for now.* As was her habit, she would leave it for the time being and work on the final edit the following day.

Still daylight and warm out at seven-thirty, Val refilled her glass and meandered out to where Andy was busy edging around the flower beds. When he turned the edger off, Val asked if he wanted anything.

"No, I'll get something when I'm done. Thanks." He got right back to the task at hand so Val wandered back inside.

Pacing around the kitchen, into her office, and back again, she couldn't shake the restlessness that followed her. Without premeditation, she reached for her cell and hit the second number in her favorites.

"Hi, Bon. Do you have any lunch plans for tomorrow? ... Great, can we meet up?" Bonnie suggested lunch at her house. "That's perfect if you're sure."

"Of course, dear. Is everything all right?"

"Yes... or maybe... I mean there's nothing serious. I think I could use a sounding board if you don't mind. Just some things I need to sort out." Val put her phone down and turned to look out the window and spoke aloud, "What *do* I want?"

CHAPTER EIGHT – BONNIE

Ginger scampered across the living room and hopped up onto her favorite chair by the window. With back paws on the arm of the chair and front paws tapping excitedly on the windowsill, she looked over her shoulder to be sure Bonnie had been alerted and gave one little bark to be certain. With a bit of training, she had learned not to bark incessantly.

"Is she here, girl?" Bonnie knew, of course, Val must have arrived, but she had to laugh at Ginger's tail wagging her whole bottom. Her four-legged ball of fur scurried down from her look-out spot and to the front door. "Okay, okay, let me get there to let her in."

"Good morning. How are you and the little one today?" Val asked, greeting her best friend with a warm hug. "No, I didn't forget you, Ginger."

The little Teacup Pomeranian jumped into Val's arms and was busy kissing her second favorite human—well maybe her third now that she'd cozied up to Joe Marconi—when Bonnie went for her treats. Val instantly became a memory as the three pounds of light orange fur waved its paws in the air and accepted its reward.

"How about a cup of tea?" Bonnie offered. Val usually stuck to her hazelnut coffee at home, but she had learned to love the tea her friend always brewed.

Bonnie brought the dainty china cups to the table, then carried the pot over and poured. All the while, she silently observed her friend's unusually quiet demeanor. "All right, my dear. Now what's troubling you?"

Val added a little sugar and moved the spoon back and forth—as she'd learned was the proper way—and stared into the steaming liquid before answering. "Nothing really."

Bonnie waited patiently for more. When her friend drew her eyes away from the tea cup, Bonnie tried to read her expression. She was usually quite good at this, but today she couldn't discern what was going on.

"Val?" Still she waited, fearing the depth of what the trouble might be.

Val drew in a deep breath and sighed, raising her head to finally look into Bonnie's eyes. "Honestly Bonnie, I don't know what's wrong with me."

"What do you mean?"

"I mean everything is fine. Seriously. I can think of absolutely no reason for me to be upset or unhappy. I have a good marriage. A good life." Bonnie saw her expression lighten as she added, "A wonderful friend." Another long pause and Val's smile melted away. "So why do I feel so empty? So restless?"

Bonnie sipped her tea unsure how to respond at first. It was hard to be analytical with her best friend, but she decided the only way to help now, might be to put her therapist hat on for a few minutes. *What would I say to a client who presented like this?*

"How long have you been feeling this way, dear? I had no idea."

"I'm not sure. I guess it's been getting gradually worse over the last six months to a year."

Bonnie thought about that for a few seconds and had an idea. "So, can you think of anything that changed in your life at about that time?" She watched Val's face for any sign of recognition. Then it came. Her friend's furrowed brow smoothed, and her eyes widened.

"You know what? That's about the time Susan got her act together and was able to be reunited with Betsy. Do you think it could have something to do with that?" she asked.

Bonnie felt pretty certain it had everything to do with that, but she didn't want to say so. "What do you think?" She could almost see the wheels turning behind Val's eyes. She remembered the tears Val had shed describing the day Betsy had taken her little suitcase and walked out Val and Andy's front door and back into her mother's arms.

"Bonnie, I think you may be onto something." Val leaned back in her chair. "Wow, I was so busy when Betsy was with us. I mean... I was exhausted most of the time, but..."

Bonnie waited for Val to continue, but she seemed stumped and simply shook her head. She lifted the tea cup to her lips before realizing it was empty.

Bonnie reached across the small table and poured from the cream and gold china teapot. "But... you had a purpose?"

"Yes! That's it. I felt needed."

"And you don't feel needed now?"

"No. I mean, well, yes, I know I'm needed, but not in the same way. Not the way Betsy needed me." Val sighed, and Bonnie decided to give her time to process this revelation by getting on with lunch when the timer signaled the quiche was ready.

"Bonnie, this is delicious," Val said. "I never would have thought to put chilled gazpacho with the quiche, but it's perfect. And you know you didn't need to go to all this trouble for me."

"Thanks, but you know I love doing it." Bonnie's lips slowly curled into a smile. "Maybe that's part of my sense of purpose." She had always loved cooking and baking, but much of the joy had gone out of it when Frank died. "This is more fun than cooking for one."

"Will you be cooking for Joe again this week?" Val asked peeking up through her lashes.

Bonnie didn't mind the teasing at all. "No, not this week. He's actually cooking for me this week. Ginger and I are invited for dinner at his place Wednesday evening."

"Oh good. You can tell me all about it when we play Thursday." Val winked. "I'm anxious to hear if he's a good cook."

"Oh, he is."

"Really?" Val picked up her dishes and carried them to the sink. "So, this isn't the first time you've had his cooking, huh? You've been holding out on me."

Bonnie realized she hadn't told Val about the other time. The time she'd found herself so bowled over by what Joe had suggested after dinner. And she wondered if his question would come up again this time. "Don't worry, Val. I'll give you all the gory details Thursday." *Well, maybe not all.*

CHAPTER NINE – SUSAN

Though Susan sometimes felt a twinge of nostalgia for her old nursing position at Madison General, she was thrilled to have found her new niche at an outpatient mental health clinic. She discovered she loved working with the mentally ill at the Adira Clinic. Especially those with a dual diagnosis and struggling with alcoholism/addiction.

It's almost as if God allowed me to go through my own addiction to prepare me for this work.

And one of the perks of this position was the hours. Working 8:00 A.M. to 3:30 P.M. Monday through Thursday meant she could be home in time to meet Elizabeth's school bus, plus she only worked until noon on Fridays. With Amber, her stay-at-home neighbor, willing to cover if she was ever detained, Susan avoided the added expense of childcare—a blessing considering her smaller paycheck.

As she parked the car in the garage, went inside, and hung her keys on the hook, Susan marveled at how her life had fallen into line once she'd realized she was powerless over her addiction to alcohol. In gratitude, she stood in the silence of her home and spoke the words of the Serenity Prayer.

The harp sounds on her cell broke the silence. Susan's jaw dropped when she checked the caller ID. "What in the world?" She answered cautiously, unsure what to expect.

"Hi, Susan. I'm sorry to bother you, but I'm calling to ask if you could do me a favor."

Val asking her for a favor? This really took Susan by surprise.

"If I can," Susan answered guardedly. "What is it?"

"I know this may sound a little crazy, but I've really been missing Bet... I mean Elizabeth, and I wondered if maybe I could pick her up one day and bring her to my house for a few hours." She talked faster and faster adding, "And I thought maybe you could have a little quiet time to yourself. Win-win?"

Susan laughed out loud. "I don't need quiet time, but I guess it wouldn't hurt." She still fretted that Val might be judging her, but she felt more relaxed each time they spoke, and Val didn't say anything snarky. Though Susan knew it would probably feel strange and a bit lonely eating alone that night, they worked out the details and ended the call in time for Susan to walk down to the bus stop and meet Elizabeth.

"Guess who called me about you, Elizabeth?"

"Daddy?" Elizabeth asked excitedly.

"No sweetie, but we'll see him soon." She saw her daughter's expression wilt and added quickly, "But Aunt Val wants to see you!" She had to swallow her resentment when she saw the child's renewed excitement. "She misses you."

"I miss her too. I love Aunt Val."

"Would you like to go to her house for a visit?" With furrowed brow, Susan studied her daughter's face when the child lowered her head and didn't respond. "What's wrong?"

"Will you come back and get me? I don't want to stay." Elizabeth's eyes questioned.

"Yes, yes, of course." Susan hurried to reassure her, realizing she must be thinking of another time. The time Susan had been incarcerated for a DUI and Elizabeth had to stay with Val and Andy for all those months.

"You don't have to go, but if you do, I promise it'll only be for a couple hours after school Wednesday. Like a play date. You'll be right back here with me before bedtime. What do you think?"

"Okay." Elizabeth's face morphed into a huge grin as she jumped up and down. "Yay!" She hopped up on the stool at the island and unpacked her backpack and lunchbox. "I didn't eat all my grapes at lunch. Can I have them now?"

"Yes, you may. I'll get you some milk, and do you want some SunChips too?"

With a mouthful of grapes, Elizabeth nodded emphatically. "Daddy has SunChips at his house now, too." She became more and more animated as she prattled on about what she and Marty would do on the weekend.

As Susan listened, a part of her brain strayed. *But this is only Monday.* Susan looked forward to seeing her ex when she dropped Elizabeth off at his house, hoping he'd invite her in again, and maybe they could spend some time together.

"I'm gonna go play now," Elizabeth said hopping down, grabbing her backpack, and dashing off to her room.

Susan wondered at her daughter's endless fount of energy as she rinsed her glass, put it in the dishwasher, and wiped the few crumbs from the counter. Gone were the days of sinks full of dirty dishes and sour milk on the counter.

Susan looked around, and seeing everything was in order, grabbed her phone and headed to her bedroom. She took off her shoes and sat on the edge of the bed, thinking. *Why not?* After a slight hesitation, she called the first number in her favorites.

"Hi, what's up?" he said.

Marty's cheerful voice put a smile on Susan's face. She'd expected to get his voicemail, but he must have been between patients.

"Yeah, I had a cancellation. The patient said she was having car trouble." Marty laughed. "That seems to be a favorite for getting out of a dentist appointment." Susan knew from all their years together it was usually new patients who chickened out. "So, what's going on? There's nothing wrong with Lizzy, is there?"

"No, she's fine." Susan heard the alarm in his voice and hurried to explain, "I just had a thought... I mean I wanted to ask if you're busy after hours Wednesday."

When he told her he'd be done with his last patient by four, she took a deep breath and plunged ahead.

She told him about their child's 'play date' with Val and ventured, "I'll be on my own and wondered if you might want to grab an early dinner?"

When he agreed without hesitation, Susan let out her breath. She could feel the silly grin on her face. The grin she couldn't erase all the while she was preparing dinner. Perhaps because now she knew Wednesday evening she would not be dining alone.

CHAPTER TEN – VAL

Val laughed, glancing at the little chatterbox in the rearview mirror. Betsy hadn't stopped talking since she'd climbed into the back of Val's car and hopped on her booster seat. She told Val about her BFF, Jordan, who was in her class, lived next door, and was so much smaller even though they were the same age. She told Val about her teacher—whom she loved—and how much she was learning. And she also talked about how her Momma and Daddy liked each other again.

"I wish he'd come back and live at our house."

Glancing at the child in the mirror again, Val saw the sudden change in her expression, but the little frown disappeared when she added, "I'm going to make another picture to give him Friday."

"Is he coming to visit on Friday?"

"No, I'm going to Daddy's 'partment for the weekend. And Daddy said we could go to the park Saturday! Momma doesn't ever take me to the park. She doesn't like it there."

Val had a pretty good idea why Susan didn't like it at the park. That's where she had been mugged a year ago. She had been so drunk when it happened that she thought she'd just passed out and hit her head. When the truth came out, she discovered a man in the park had seen her as an easy mark, knocked her out, and stolen her wallet and car. That very car was in a hit and run accident overnight. Having blacked out—with no memory of the prior night's events—Susan believed she must have been the driver.

It wasn't until the police caught the scum who'd left his victim to die and brought him to trial that the whole truth came out. She was even more horrified when she discovered the victim was Marty's uncle, Joe Marconi. That had been a wake-up call for Susan who finally acknowledged she needed help and she was indeed an alcoholic. She'd been in recovery and attending Alcoholics Anonymous meetings ever since. Val was amazed at the change in the woman who'd been so out of control.

The little voice in the backseat interrupted her reverie. "Aunt Val, did you hear me?"

"I'm sorry, sweetie. What did you say?"

"Maybe you should turn the radio down so you can hear me better," Betsy said a little flippantly. "I said let's play a game."

The rest of the ride was filled with taking turns calling out words that began with whatever letter the child chose. She always won, of course.

Val finally pulled into the garage, killed the engine, and blew out her breath in an exhausted sigh. *Now I remember why I was so tired all the time.* But she also realized how much she had missed this.

"Can I have a snack?"

Betsy had charged ahead and was already perched on a stool at the big center island. Val obliged her with some cheese and crackers which she practically inhaled.

Talking through the final cracker she asked, "Do you still have my toy box in your office?"

"I sure do." Val hadn't had the heart to get rid of the storage ottoman filled with toys, puppets, puzzles, and coloring books—things Betsy loved to play with—when she'd gone back to live with her mother. Before she could say 'let's go' to her little playmate, the child had dashed ahead. Val hurried after her, laughing, and almost ran into Betsy who had stopped short just inside the entrance.

She stood motionless staring up at the wall.

Val's eyes followed to find the object of her attention. "Oh, you're looking at Mia's latest drawing. Do you like it?" Val came around to face the child and was shocked by the expression she saw there. Val fell to her knees in front of Betsy, and asked, "Honey, what's wrong?"

"That's where the scary man is." Betsy's chin quivered as she spoke.

Val pulled the child into her arms. "Oh sweetie, it's just a picture. It's okay." She felt the child trembling in her embrace.

"But I saw him. That's his house."

"Come sit on my lap." She sat right there on the floor holding Betsy until she was calm.

When it seemed safer, she asked, "Now, Betsy, what scary man were you talking about? Whose house does it look like?"

"It *is* his house. I saw it."

"Can you tell me where?"

"In my bad dream. I saw him. And that was his house."

"Sweetie, there are lots of houses like that one. Mia just made this one up. You know... like the other drawings you've seen her do. I'm sorry it scared you."

"But that has to be his house," Betsy said peeking over Val's shoulder. " 'Cuz that's his truck."

Val looked at the blue truck. She couldn't understand why, but shuddered with a sudden chill.

Chapter Eleven – Susan

Pulling into the parking lot of Chez Celina, Susan was flooded with melancholy. She stared at the café where she and Marty had shared so many singular moments in their courtship and marriage. *How could I have thrown all that away? What was I thinking?*

She shook off her wistfulness and checked her appearance in the rearview mirror as soon as she spotted Marty pulling in. Drawing her honey-blonde hair back, she was glad she'd taken the time to redo her makeup and accent her crystal blue eyes—a feature Marty claimed had grabbed his attention and stolen his heart.

Marty parked, waved, and hurried to greet her, and she felt her heart quicken in her chest just as it had when they first started dating.

He hasn't aged a bit.

She loved the way he'd let his wavy red hair grow—reminded her of a Scottish rogue—and how he always had the slightest auburn five-o'clock shadow. And those sea blue eyes that looked bluer because of his hair. *God, he's sexy!*

Susan sucked in her breath, half afraid she'd spoken out loud as she stepped out of the car. And did she imagine it, or was his usual greeting hug a little tighter... and did it last a little longer? She inhaled the scent that was uniquely Marty, and her face felt much hotter than one might expect from the May sun.

"It's good to see you, Suze," he said holding her at arm's length and giving her his most charming smile. "This was a great idea."

"I'm glad you could make it. I'm not used to having dinner without Elizabeth, and this will be a lot nicer than eating alone."

"Oh, so I'm just filling in for our daughter, huh?"

Alarmed, Susan's mouth opened to deny his accusation, but she snapped it shut again when she saw the merriment spread across his face, then laughed with him.

Once inside, Marty noticed it was available and asked for the very table where he'd proposed sixteen years earlier. Susan wondered if he remembered. She wondered if he recalled the details of that extraordinary night as clearly as she did. The tiny diamond ring he'd slipped on her finger—all he could afford when just starting his dental practice—was to her the most magnificent gem she'd ever seen. She unconsciously rubbed the inside of her empty ring finger on her left hand.

Marty ordered two iced teas, unlike the wine they'd had before his proposal, and their dinner conversation certainly didn't resemble that night as it now centered primarily around their daughter.

It wasn't until Marty asked if she wanted dessert and she declined that the conversation took a turn.

"Susan, a lot has happened in the past couple years. A lot's changed. We've both changed." Susan listened and nodded in agreement, barely breathing—wondering what he was getting at. "I don't know about you, Suze, but I've been doing a lot of thinking about where we go from here." Marty took a deep breath. "Finding out, you know, finding out that Lizzy wasn't really my daughter, well that's not something you can easily get past."

Oh God, no. "Marty, I'm so sorry. If I could undo what I did that night..." She remembered the look in his eyes when she'd shouted 'Elizabeth isn't your daughter!' and the blank expression on his face that had morphed into shock and disbelief. It was an image printed indelibly in her memory. A picture she could never erase.

"No, stop, Susan. Don't apologize again. We've been through all that." His head was bowed low as he shook it and held up his hand. When he raised it and looked at her again, she saw him blink back tears. Her worst fear was going to be realized. She dreaded his next words, afraid he would say he didn't want to see her anymore. *But we've been getting along so well.*

"Susan, I don't care anymore. I mean Lizzy *is* my daughter, and you're her mother, and I love you both."

Susan gasped. She couldn't believe she'd heard right. Watching him get out of his seat and get down on one knee—just as he had sixteen years before—she couldn't breathe.

"Susan, I don't ask this lightly, but I know I don't want to spend my life with anyone but you. Will you marry me... again?"

Susan tried to choke back the tears but to no avail. She struggled to find her voice, but when it wouldn't come, she nodded vigorously.

As Marty rose from his knee, she jumped into his arms oblivious to the stares.

"I'm not done, you know," he said, reaching into his pocket. He slid the beautiful marquis-cut diamond onto her finger, and they both laughed and cried as they became aware of the other diners who were now applauding.

Their waiter appeared carrying a bottle of sparkling cider and the couple toasted their engagement and decided dessert was in order after all. Since Val wasn't to bring Elizabeth home until eight o'clock, they still had a little time, but as soon as she finished the last spoonful of her butter pecan ice cream, Susan was ready to go.

"I can't wait to tell Elizabeth, but I think we should do it together. Do you want to come back to the house with me now?"

"I have a better idea." Marty wore a sly smile. "How about we keep our little secret until Friday when you bring her to my place?"

"Well, okay, but why?"

"Trust me. I have a plan. I was hoping you'd say yes and planned ahead for a special way of sharing it with our Lizzy-Elizabeth."

Susan had to laugh at that. She hadn't heard him call her his funny combo name in a long, long time. She finally agreed, knowing it would be a hard secret to keep, and grudgingly said goodbye at the car. But not until they'd shared a kiss. Not one of the usual friendly kisses they'd been sharing lately, but a kiss that said I want more... and I want it forever.

Chapter Twelve – Kathy

"I'd like to introduce myself," Kathy said, taking the time to make eye contact with each of the other women sitting around the card table. She could see by their curious looks, they were intrigued by her statement. After all, they'd known Kathy James for years now.

When she could no longer hold it in, she laughed, then announced, "My name is now Kathy A. Stark!"

It was Val who finally broke the baffled silence. "What are you talking about, girl? I thought you might go back to your maiden name, but that wasn't 'Stark'."

"Nope. I was glad to get rid of that name when I married the asshole—sorry ladies, pardon my language—but now I don't want it either. So, I picked one of my own, and I think it's a name that will look great on the front of my book when it's released this summer."

The little room erupted into joyous chaos at this announcement, just as she imagined it would. They all knew she'd finished writing her mystery novel, but ever since she discovered the cheating husband and filed for divorce, she hadn't talked much about it.

Val, the only person in the bridge group she'd allowed to read it, was the first to jump up and embrace her. "Congratulations! Oh my gosh, that's wonderful. I'm so happy for you." Then everyone was on their feet with the cards totally forgotten for the moment.

"Is that why we have these lovely wine glasses on the table, dear?" Bonnie asked. "It seems there's a toast in order."

Kathy responded with her mischievous smile. "You got me." She winked and disappeared into the kitchen, returning seconds later with a chilled bottle of Champagne, and more laughter erupted with the popping of the cork. She filled the four glasses, flashed an enormous smile, and said, "Here's to me!"

"Oh, c'mon. We can do better than that," Sarah said. "May I?" With everyone's agreement, she continued. "I know you've been working on this for a long time, and we're all so very proud of you. Here's to your book release and it being a best-seller."

Val, who had read and helped edit the book (all but the dedication and acknowledgments), cheered the loudest. "And why am I just hearing about this?" she asked good-humoredly.

"Actually... I only found out yesterday. And you know me, had to go for the dramatic announcement. Now, I think you guys came here to play cards. We'd better get started before I get a delay of game penalty." Kathy was beginning to get a little embarrassed by all the attention.

"One more question," Val said as they took their seats. "Why Stark?"

"It means strong," was Kathy's simple reply. She had felt defeated and nearly crumbled upon discovering her husband's infidelity. But with a new resolve, she was determined to throw off the mantle of weakness and take control of her life once more. "I'm kind of reinventing myself. I'm even toying with the idea of moving to New York. My sister said I could stay in her walk-up until I find a place of my own."

"Oh my, that is exciting!" Bonnie said. "But we certainly would miss you here at the bridge table."

Kathy felt a twinge of guilt and quickly added, "Well, nothing is definite yet."

"All right, but getting back to your new name," Val said after Kathy assured them she was still in the 'thinking it over' stage. "You've piqued my curiosity. What does the 'A' stand for?"

"Okay, don't laugh... It stands for *Alzena*." She saw her friends exchange glances and thought she should explain. "It means imaginative, creative, and longing for freedom. I wanted to pick a name that, you know, stood for something." She looked to Val for approval and was relieved to see her smile.

"I think it's perfect."

The cards were dealt, and bidding went round the table, ending with a three-no-trump bid by Sarah. As dummy, Kathy knew her hand should assure her partner would win the contract, so she excused herself for a well-needed break.

After washing her hands, she grabbed the hand towel to dry them and looked at the words tattooed on her inner arm. She'd had them permanently placed there not long after she lost her mother to cancer and was left caring for her drunken father.

You are stronger than you think!

Kathy had often needed to look at those words when she felt hopeless and defeated. Her father had let her down. Her husband had let her down. She decided her happiness would never again be dependent on a man.

Raising her eyes to the mirror, she lifted her chin and affirmed, *I am enough. I'm going to make you proud, Kathy Alzena Stark. I am enough!*

CHAPTER THIRTEEN – SARAH

Sarah had no trouble winning the three-no-trump contract and gave her partner an appreciative smile when Kathy returned from the bathroom. "That was fun, Ms. Stark," she said. "Our hands were a perfect match. And we got one overtrick. Bam!" Everyone laughed at the good-hearted taunt as she slid the cards across the table. Heaving a huge sigh, she shook her head.

"What's that about?" Val tilted her own head inquisitively at her daughter-in-law.

Sarah pulled up her chin and sighed. "I think I really needed this tonight."

"Is something wrong, dear?" Bonnie asked.

"No, no. Life is good. No complaints here. I'm just tired. The kids are great, and they help out when I ask, but they are kids... and there are five of them now." Sarah chuckled. "It's been a long time since I had a baby to take care of. I think I'd forgotten how much work they can be." She explained that Craig was always willing to help, but sometimes Destiny just wanted her momma. What she didn't add was that there was more wearing her out than the children.

Sarah couldn't escape the daunting thoughts that kept popping into her brain when she least expected them. Earlier in the day she'd had another phone call from Holly, and her former client seemed more agitated than the last time they'd spoken.

"Sarah, I don't think he's taking his meds anymore. I mean he doesn't even sound rational."

Sarah had tried to calm Holly and asked if her ex still had a key to their place and whether she believed he might come there to hurt her again.

"No, no... it's you I'm worried about! He keeps going on and on about how you've ruined his life. How you turned me against

him. Honestly Sarah, it's like he's totally consumed by the idea that if it weren't for you we'd still be together."

Sarah had done her best to put Holly's mind at ease and assure her there was nothing to worry about, but convincing herself was more challenging.

"It's your bid, dear." Bonnie's voice snapped Sarah out of her reverie, and she realized she had yet to put her cards in order.

"Oops, sorry about that." She scrambled to arrange the suits and made a quick one-club bid. Looking to her left, she saw her mother-in-law's drawn brow.

"Are you sure you're okay, Sarah?" Val asked.

"Nothing a good night's sleep can't cure," she lied.

At the end of the night—with Val and Bonnie victorious once more—Val admonished her daughter-in-law to get some rest and let Craig help more with the baby. Sarah assured her she would and that it was no big deal.

Then, before getting in her car, she took a quick look up and down the street. No signs of a blue pickup. *Sarah, get a grip.*

Arriving home, Sarah scanned the street, and seeing no headlights and no strange vehicles parked on their cul-de-sac, pulled into the garage.

***

It was several seconds later that the car Sarah had been searching for turned off its headlights and eased onto the dead-end street with the five huge homes. The grandest—the one the driver looked at with disdain—was the Reed residence.

This wasn't the first time Ben had been on this street, though it had taken him a while to find out where the bitch lived. He'd tried a Google search to no avail. All he could find on her was the address for the agency where she worked. But that was enough. With persistence he'd finally seen her leaving the office one afternoon and followed her. It took a couple tries to at last discover where she lived. But he was cunning. He knew if he followed her

56

partway and turned off, he could watch for her another day and pick up from there.

After just three tries, Holly's ex knew exactly where Sarah Reed lived, and with a little more research, patience and persistence, he'd learned all about her family and their habits. He knew the older kids' names. He knew when Sarah was home alone. He even knew where her children went to school and when they got home.

Benjamin Garfield, Jr., was almost ready to get his revenge.

He watched the house for more than an hour. Watched until one by one the windows went dark. As the warm glow vanished, leaving the house in near total darkness, Ben smirked. *You ruined my life, bitch. Well, soon you're gonna pay!*

With the full moon shining brightly behind it, the Reed residence showed no evidence of the peaceful family within. It suddenly emerged as a dark, gloomy silhouette. But not as dark as the seething storm of malevolence in Ben Garfield's eyes.

***

Sarah pushed back the quilt cover and quietly slid out of bed. She'd been fighting the uneasy feeling in the pit of her stomach since turning off the bedside lamp. Craig snored softly, and so as not to disturb him, she tiptoed through the darkness and headed toward her children's bedrooms.

The nightlights were all she needed to see that baby Destiny was sleeping peacefully, as were Bobby and Cody. But approaching the girls' rooms her anxiety grew. She found Julie snoozing under her covers—which were pulled up over her head as usual—and gently drew back the coverlet to gaze at her sweet face. All was well with Julie. She could feel it.

But when Sarah got to Mia, she found the girl tossing restlessly with covers flung all about. As Sarah hauled the sheet and quilt into place, Mia's eyes popped wide open, unseeing and filled with fear.

"Honey, what's wrong? It's okay... I'm right here," Sarah spoke softly to calm her.

Mia—suddenly seeing her mother—threw her arms around her neck. "I'm s-s-scared, Mom." Her voice cracked, and Sarah could see she was on the brink of tears.

"Oh honey, you're okay. Was it another one of those dreams?" She felt Mia nod her head which was now tucked under her mother's chin. The child was shaking. "Can you tell me about it?"

Mia drew back and shook her head. "I... I can't remember, but... but I know I was so afraid."

It had been like this so many nights lately. Mia could never hold onto the dream long enough to remember what happened. But she knew it was bad.

"Mom, it just felt so evil."

Sarah said a little prayer and stroked her daughter's brow until the girl finally fell back to sleep. Though she was approaching her teen years, Mia looked so tiny and vulnerable lying there. It wasn't until Sarah tiptoed back down the hall that she heard a car engine start. *That's odd.*

Living on such a quiet cul-de-sac and being quite familiar with the families in the other four houses, she knew they were all usually settled for the night by this late hour. Hoping there was nothing wrong, she hurried to a front window and pulled back the curtain.

All the other homes were surrounded with the darkness of a slumbering neighborhood. The only movement she saw was the taillights of a vehicle as it vanished around the corner.

CHAPTER FOURTEEN – MIA

"Morning, Mom." Mia grabbed a seat and one of the pancakes stacked high in front of her. "What?" she asked noticing the odd expression on her mother's face.

"Nothing. Are you feeling better this morning?"

"Better than what?" Mia was, at first, totally confused by the question. After all, she wasn't sick and hadn't had one of her headaches in ages.

"Better than last night. Remember?"

"Oh that," Mia said as the light dawned. "I had another one of those stupid dreams, didn't I?" Seeing her mother nod, she looked toward the ceiling trying to recall what the nightmare had been about, but her memory was blank. She had too much on her mind and was way too excited to worry about it. "Oh well, no big deal. Sorry, did I wake you?"

"No, I was just peeking in on you, and you woke up looking like you'd seen a ghost," her mom said setting a glass of orange juice by her plate.

"I ain't afraid of no ghost!"

Her mother rolled her eyes, and Mia laughed at the reaction.

"Ghost Busters!" Bobby proclaimed just catching the end of the conversation.

Before long, the stack of hotcakes began to shrink as the population of the kitchen grew. They all loved Friday mornings since Mom didn't go into the office until 10:00... thus it was sticky, syrupy pancake day.

Dad was the last to arrive in the kitchen and found one lonely flapjack.

Mia saw the look of dismay on his face and couldn't resist a little teasing. "Ya snooze, ya lose, Dad!"

Above all the laughter, Mom called that more were on the way and carried in a plate stacked high.

Cody and Bobby were the first to finish, carry their plates to the kitchen, and put them in the dishwasher. Then as the girls finished up, Mom asked, "Julie, do you have band practice this afternoon?"

"Affirmative!"

"Oh, that reminds me," Mia said turning the friendship bracelet Betsy had made for her round and round. "I'll be late today, too."

"Why, what's going on with you?" Dad asked with raised eyebrows.

"A couple of the kids in my art class are having trouble with perspective, and I said I'd stay and help them this afternoon." Mia didn't like deceiving her parents, but it would be worth it.

"Seems like that should be your teacher's job... but okay." Dad shrugged. "So, will you be getting the activities bus home, or do you need a ride?"

Mia had known they'd ask so she was prepared. "As much trouble as this one girl is having, it might take a while so she said her mom would give us a ride home."

Eventually, Mia knew they'd find out the truth, but when she explained everything she was sure they wouldn't mind at all. Actually, they would be thrilled. And so proud. *It will be all right.*

Her habit of spinning her bracelet when nervous caught her mother's attention. "Mia, I know you love that because Betsy made it for you, but don't you think you've about worn it out?" Mom asked. "It looks like it's hanging on by a thread."

"No worries," Mia answered. "I'll get another piece of yarn and fix it later."

As soon as she'd cleared her place, Mia hurried back to her room, gathered up her books, and picked up her large oyster-grey art portfolio. It had been her favorite present on her last birthday and she was especially glad it was waterproof when she glanced out the window at the misty morning rain.

"C'mon, kids," Dad called. "You don't want to miss your bus." They were fortunate the school bus stopped at the end of their street so they didn't need a ride to meet it even in bad weather.

"Are you taking your whole portfolio?" Mom asked. "Do you really need all that?"

"Well, uh, I wanted to take some examples to show the kids I'm helping, and I, uh, didn't really have time to go through them. It's no big deal."

One lie just leads to another, but it'll be okay. She couldn't tell them why it was so important to have all of her best work with her. Like the man said, that would spoil the surprise. What was it his last email said? Oh yeah, he warned her to keep it a secret until they knew for sure. Yet he had seemed certain her work would qualify.

Mia reassured herself it would all be worth it as she dashed out the door and into the brewing summer storm.

CHAPTER FIFTEEN – MIA

Mia's breathing came faster and faster as she opened the girls' bathroom door just wide enough to listen for any sound of movement in the hall. There was none. Pushing the door wider, she stuck her head around the corner and scanned the empty corridor.

She saw light shining from many of the classroom doors, including the art room, but Mia wasn't planning on seeing any teachers... at least not if she could help it. Holding tightly to her portfolio she measured the distance and counted the classrooms she must pass to reach the double doors leading out of the building.

Mia knew if she ran, it would only draw attention, and that's one thing she didn't need right now. Taking one more deep breath, she boldly and briskly made her way to the exit. She didn't look back—nor side to side—as she headed across the parking lot to the sidewalk.

I'm not doing anything wrong. Though she tried to convince herself that was true, lying to her parents had tied a knot in Mia's gut. There had been little white lies, of course, when she was younger, but even then, her guilt had usually led to tears and a pitiful confession. And, naturally, she was always forgiven. *Besides, I can tell them everything as soon as it's definite.*

Mia hurried along the sidewalk, crossed the bridge onto Monroe Avenue, and saw the silver Mercedes parked just where his email said it would be, in front of the old elementary school that had been converted into a carpet store.

Mia hesitated.

Something didn't seem right. *But this is an opportunity of a lifetime.* She couldn't blow it just because of a silly feeling.

Bending down to peer through the passenger side window, Mia saw Mr. Benson reach across and open the door for her. Mia wavered for a moment. She was getting in a car with a complete stranger. *What if...*

"Hi, Mia. You are Mia Reed, the next great artist to set the world on fire, right? I'm Harold Benson. Hop in. You can put your portfolio in the back."

Still Mia faltered.

Benson smiled and said, "We don't want to be late for our appointment with Mr. Phelps, do we?"

Mia knew Timothy Phelps was the agent responsible for helping several unknown artists become quite known. She couldn't believe she was actually going to meet him and get to show him her work. After she placed the portfolio in the back, she slid into the Mercedes and fastened her seatbelt.

Mia could feel herself perspiring—another gift of puberty—and her hands were shaking. With a sidelong glance at the driver, she asked, "Do you really think he'll like my drawings?"

Benson didn't answer at first, and then gave a quick, "Sure."

They rode along in silence, Mia becoming more uneasy with each passing moment.

They seemed to be driving away from the town. "Um, where is Mr. Phelps' office?" No response. Mia wiped her sweaty palms on the skirt of her sundress. She had wanted to dress up more professionally to meet the agent who would make her famous but feared it would raise suspicion. "How far is it?"

"Don't worry about it," was all Benson said.

When Mia turned to look at him, she saw he wasn't smiling like before. The knot in her stomach squeezed tighter. "I, I thought Mr. Phelps' office was in Madison." No answer. "This road goes away from Madison," she said barely above a whisper.

Benson turned onto the highway and accelerated.

"Where are you t-t-taking me?" Mia heard the quiver in her voice and tried to reason away the panic threatening to consume her. *Maybe it's in Johnstown. But why doesn't he answer me? Yes!*

Benson turned the Mercedes onto the exit for Johnstown, and Mia was flooded with relief. But before reaching the main part of town, he took a fork in the road... and he was driving much too fast.

Mia had no concept of the time, but he seemed to be driving farther and farther into the country. Mia rode in silence with dread, and the smile of the man with brown hair had turned into more of a sneer. The only sound was the tires on the road and the voice screaming in her head, *God, help me! I'm so stupid! Please, God, help me!*

Her dread turned to alarm when the nefarious driver turned onto a dirt road leading up a steep incline. They were in the middle of nowhere. There were miles and miles of twists and turns. Mia recognized she was completely lost. Completely alone.

"Almost there."

At the sound of his voice, Mia pulled closer to the car door, putting as much space between her and the stranger as possible.

He turned and looked at her for the first time since they'd left the highway. It was a menacing look that turned Mia's fear to terror. Unable to hold them back any longer, tears streamed down Mia's face.

"Please take me home." The words she had wanted to scream, came out as a whimper.

The man who called himself Benson drove across a rickety bridge and pulled through a clump of trees revealing what she assumed was some kind of hunting camp. He put on the emergency brake, got out, and strode around the front of the car. When he yanked open the passenger side, Mia tried to pull away, but he grabbed her by the wrist and jerked her out of the car so hard, she lost her footing.

He obviously didn't care. She stumbled to her feet and scanned the area trying to get her bearings. Trying to think. Trying to find her way out.

But there was no escape. Mia saw nothing but woods surrounding an A-frame cabin that looked eerily familiar. Then she realized why. *That's the cabin. I drew this!*

The cruel stranger dragged her toward the chalet—the only one in sight—and up the steps, shoving her through the door.

When she fell, he yelled, "Get up! Get over there! And quit your sniveling!"

Mia scrambled to her feet. "Please, I just want to go home. I won't tell anyone..."

"You're not going anywhere," he roared. Then he took a breath and blew it out slowly. "Now look, I'm not going to hurt you. Not if you behave yourself." He walked to the tiny refrigerator at the end of the row of cabinets and pulled out a pitcher of water. "Are you thirsty?"

"No," she murmured, "but I have to go to the bathroom." Mia's face flushed, and she prayed he would let her go before she peed her pants.

He grabbed her by the arm—not quite as rough as the last time—and pushed her into a hallway with two doors. Through one she saw the bathroom. Through the other she saw a bed. She stopped short.

"What are you doin'? I thought you had to go."

Looking over her shoulder, Mia entered the bathroom. She started to close the door.

"No," he hissed. "The door stays open. Don't worry, I ain't interested in watchin'. I'm not some kind of perv." He turned his back, but he didn't walk away.

Mia finally managed to relieve herself, and, red-faced, she told him she was done.

He pushed her back into the big room that seemed to serve as kitchen and living room and toward an overstuffed couch. "Stop your bawlin' and sit down."

It wasn't a request; it was an order. When she didn't comply immediately, he put his brawny hands on her shoulders and pushed her down.

"Here, drink this."

Mia's hand shook as she raised the glass of water to her lips. It had a slightly funny taste that drew her eyes up in suspicion.

"What? There's nothing wrong with the water here."

"I... I'm not thirsty."

"I said drink it!"

Mia looked up at Benson hovering over her with danger in his eyes, and she drank. "Why are you doing this?" she asked meekly.

"To teach her a lesson," he grumbled.

Frightened and confused, Mia felt herself drifting away. *Who is he talking about? What's happening to me? Oh God, was the water poisoned?* She wanted to ask her captor, but the words were lost as she slipped into the darkness.

CHAPTER SIXTEEN – SUSAN

"Do you need help with your seatbelt?"

"No Momma, I can do it myself," Elizabeth said with utter exasperation.

Susan smiled with satisfaction at her daughter's expression of independence. The child had clung so tightly to her when they were first reunited—like Elizabeth was afraid she'd lose her again—but trust had gradually grown. The old fear of losing her momma only peeked out occasionally these days.

"Did you bring the picture you made for Daddy?"

"Uh-huh, it's in my backpack. And I put more hearts on it, too."

There was a long pause, and Susan glanced in the rearview mirror. It was rare that Elizabeth's chatter slowed at all this soon after school. "What's wrong, sweetie?"

Susan noticed the little crease between her daughter's brows. But the worried look vanished as quickly as it had appeared... chased by a little shoulder shrug.

"Oh, and guess what else? I brought my new book to read to him." Elizabeth talked her mother's ears off for the rest of the ride, barely taking time to catch her breath. She was even more animated than on the average day with the excitement of an overnight visit with Marty.

Elizabeth had everything she needed for the weekend, but she didn't know Susan also had placed an overnight bag for herself in the trunk earlier.

***

"You're staying and having supper with us? Really?" Elizabeth's jaw had dropped at the news before her expression morphed into sheer delight and she threw her arms around Susan.

69

Returning her daughter's hug, Susan looked over her head and smiled at Marty who was leaning against the fridge. He had added Lizzy's latest drawing to the crowded front of the appliance with tiny letter magnets. Susan thought he really should weed out some of the older pictures but knew he hated to part with any of them. He'd lost too much time with his little girl.

Susan pushed her child to arm's length and looked at the big grin which held even more charm than ever since Elizabeth had lost those front teeth. "Yes, sweetie, we're all having dinner together tonight, and I bet Daddy fixed something you really like, too."

"Um, well, it's nothing fancy, but if I remember correctly, I think my little girl likes spaghetti and meatballs. And garlic bread." Marty and Susan couldn't help laughing at Elizabeth's reaction.

This was definitely her favorite, and she appeared to thoroughly enjoy every big bite she stuffed into her little mouth. She was so busy gobbling down her spaghetti and the special little meatballs—she even found room for her salad and garlic bread— she barely stopped to talk. That is until she dropped her fork onto the plate and proclaimed she was 'filled up' and couldn't eat another bite. Her spaghetti face said it all.

"Okay, wipe your mouth, and you may be excused," Susan said then looked at Marty to see if she'd spoken out of turn. After all, this was his home.

He smiled and nodded his agreement.

"Can I watch one of my shows now?" Elizabeth looked at Susan, who looked at Marty. And once again he nodded.

"Sure Lizzy, one show, okay?"

"Yay, okay," she shouted over her shoulder, running to the living room and grabbing the remote. The child no sooner found the latest episode of *Wild Kratts* than she was totally absorbed.

Susan grabbed some of the plates and carried them to the kitchen with Marty right behind her. She didn't realize how closely behind until she felt his arms go around her and his soft kisses on the back of her neck.

"I've missed this," he said.

"Me too," Susan murmured, relishing the warmth of his touch. His hot breath stirred a fire within her, but she gently pulled away. Their little girl was much too close to let that desire get out of hand. "No, Marty..." she looked past him toward the doorway.

"What?" Marty checked behind him. "Don't worry. Lizzy's into her show. Anyway, what's wrong with her seeing us together? She's gonna know soon, and she's gonna be thrilled. It's what she wants."

"You're right, I know. It is what she wants." Susan touched his cheek then stepped back.

"It's what I want too, Suze. Everything's finally gonna be like it used to be. It will be like this whole nightmare never happened. We can forget—"

"Momma, Daddy... Come here, quick!"

CHAPTER SEVENTEEN – SARAH

"Isn't Mia home yet?" her husband asked as he kissed Sarah on the back of her neck.

She leaned her head back to accept a proper kiss before answering, "No, but I think we'd better go ahead and start dinner. They must be working longer than she expected... but Mia said one of the other kid's parents would bring her home when they're done. Should be soon." Sarah glanced at the clock on the microwave. "Oh, it really is getting late. I can't imagine they're still at the school this late. Do you think I should call her?"

"Nah, you know she'll say you're embarrassing her if you do. Why don't you just text and ask if she's on her way?"

"Yeah, good idea," Sarah said reaching for her phone, but before she even got it opened, she heard a ruckus in the family room that sounded like trouble.

She dropped the phone on the counter and hurried in to check on what she now assumed was another fight between the boys. Sarah didn't know what had gotten into them lately, but they were always going at it. Typically, it was just a lot of yelling back and forth, but occasionally it developed into punches and rolling around in a knock-down drag-out fight if no one stepped in to break it up.

Oh great. And right before dinner.

By the time Sarah got to the scene of the action Craig had already stepped in. "Knock it off," he boomed. "That's enough. What's wrong with you two? You know better!"

"He started it!" Bobby yelled.

"I don't give a damn who started it!"

Both boys stopped short and their jaws dropped. Sarah wasn't sure if it had been their father's tone of voice or the fact that he swore—something almost unheard of from Craig—but whichever it was, the effect was sobering.

The boys weren't the only ones to react. Seeing the fear in her sons' eyes and the anger in her husband's, Sarah spoke quietly. "Okay, everybody take a deep breath."

Craig shot her a look she interpreted to mean *I've got this*, but she knew the situation needed to be defused.

"Dinner is ready so, Bobby, go wash your hands in your bathroom. Cody, use the sink in the kitchen. We'll discuss this after dinner."

Julie rolled her eyes and returned to the kitchen to grab and carry in the vegetables. "*Boys*," she said with utter disdain.

"Shh." Sarah didn't need her to get in on the act. "But, yeah, *boys...*" she said conspiratorially and winked her agreement.

As they gathered around the table, Craig asked, "Whose turn is it to say grace?"

Julie spoke up and began even before her brothers had bowed their heads. "Lord, bless this food we are about to receive and the hands that prepared it. We give thanks for the many blessings we have... and pray that Bobby and Cody will learn to get along. Amen."

Sarah opened her eyes and didn't miss the smug smile on her oldest daughter's face... or the glare her youngest brother sent Julie's way. Bobby looked like he could barely contain himself.

Everyone ate in silence for a while—an unusual state of affairs for this family full of children with so much to say, they usually talked over each other—until Cody finally broke the silence.

"Where's Mia?"

"Oh, she stayed late to help some kids with their art projects," Julie answered.

Sarah realized texting Mia had completely flown out of her mind with the earlier uproar.

"Did she answer your text?" Craig asked.

It was the first time he'd really looked at her since she interrupted his earlier tirade, and she was relieved to see no signs of lingering anger on his face.

"No, I didn't finish the text. I was sort of distracted," she said with a sidelong glance at the boys. She noticed Cody seemed oblivious as his fork flew from plate to mouth nearly with the speed of light. Bobby, however, moved his food around the plate barely eating—very unusual for him. "Bobby, what's wrong? Why aren't you eating?"

"Because he's a big baby," Cody shot back.

"That's enough!" Craig said before Sarah could even react.

"I hate you!" Bobby yelled at his brother then jumped out of his seat and headed for his room.

"Sorry," Cody mumbled. "But he is."

Sarah moved to get up and follow her son—as was her natural inclination—but Craig told her to give Bobby some space and finish her dinner. She did her best but didn't have much appetite.

As soon as she'd managed the last bite, Sarah excused herself and, carrying Bobby's untouched plate, headed for his room. She found him lying on his back staring at the ceiling.

"What's going on, kiddo?" She sat on the edge of his bed and wondered at how her baby boy had grown so quickly. "Hey, don't let Cody get to you. You know he doesn't mean it."

"Yeah, he does. And he's not that much older." Bobby rolled over to face the window "He thinks he's so tough just 'cuz he's bigger."

"Well, *I know* you boys love each other even if you don't. Here, I brought you your dinner. Why don't you eat something, and you'll feel better?" Sarah was certain he wanted to continue pouting, but he rolled back over and sat up when his appetite got the better of him. "Just bring your dishes to the kitchen when you're done," she said ruffling his hair.

When she turned to leave, Sarah was surprised to find Cody standing in the doorway.

"Sorry, Bobby."

Sarah heard the sincerity in his voice this time, and so did Bobby.

"It's okay," her youngest son replied.

Content that her boys would be okay now—until the next time—Sarah headed for the kitchen where she found Craig and Julie cleaning up and her phone right where she'd left it.

"Still no Mia?" she asked, and with the negative reply shot off a text.

It's getting late. Are you on the way home?

"Sounds like Dessie's getting a little restless," Julie said. "Do you want me to get her?"

"No, finish helping your dad here. I need to get Destiny in the bath." Sarah laid the phone down to retrieve the fussy baby and only checked for the return message when she finally had her settled for the night.

Spending the night with a friend.

Sarah stared at the text in disbelief. *What friend?*

She went to the window and stared out at the darkness. This wasn't like Mia at all. She quickly hit her favorites and called her daughter's phone. *No way.* No answer... straight to voicemail.

Sarah found Craig in the family room.

He looked up at her, and his smile faded. "What's wrong?"

"I wish I knew. It's Mia." Sarah frowned. "She's not coming home."

CHAPTER EIGHTEEN – MIA

Mia awoke to total darkness. Slowly, as her eyes adjusted, she scanned her surroundings. Recognizing nothing, she was struck with a sudden realization. This wasn't her room. This wasn't her house. Panic grabbed her by the throat.

She didn't remember going home or going to bed. *No, I... I was going to see that agent...*

Mia fought through the fog, searching for answers. And gradually memory of the events of the day crept back into awareness. But with them came no relief—only dread.

Through a haze she remembered Benson... and the water with the slightly bitter taste. And she remembered hearing the swoosh that signaled a new text on her phone. *But I couldn't answer.* She'd been paralyzed and sinking into a black hole.

Mia struggled to get up, but she was still paralyzed. No. She was restrained. That explained the aching in her wrists and ankles. With great effort Mia managed to swing her legs off the couch, but when her feet touched the floor, she knew she wouldn't be able to walk. She searched frantically for her phone, but it was gone. *He took it!*

She wanted to scream yet was terrified to even make a sound. *Where is he?*

The first sign of dawn was breaking in the sky. The sun wasn't up, but she could see the sky had begun to brighten, and though the café curtains on the windows shut out most of the view, the orangish hue signaled the coming sunrise and Mia realized she'd been here all night.

Examining her wrists and ankles in the dim light, she was bewildered by her restraints. She wasn't tied with rope like she would have expected. *What the hell?* It was some kind of cloth—like ripped up clothing—wound all around and back and forth with long black zip ties threaded through and secured. She couldn't move.

But I could cut them off. Scissors... or a knife.

Mia inched herself forward, pulling with her heels as she scooted her bottom to the edge of the couch. Then she eased herself down to the floor. She glanced toward the hallway that led back to the bedroom and bathroom. There was no sound. Barely breathing, she edged her way slowly toward the kitchen where she hoped to find a knife.

She didn't know where she'd go from there, but first things first. One of the zip ties dug into her right ankle, and she was soaked with sweat but she continued to pull with her heels and edge toward the kitchen area until she heard the tires rolling on the dirt road outside.

A quick glimmer of hope jumped into her mind. *Dad?* Then, as quickly as it came, the hope was dashed. How could her parents possibly know where to find her? She didn't even know where she was.

Mia stiffened at the sound of a key in the lock. Then the door opened, and she was blinded by a bright beam of a flashlight.

"What the hell?" The man slammed the door behind him and moved toward her. "Damn! What in the hell do you think you're doing?"

She recognized the voice. Benson. Cringing in fear she whimpered.

"I asked you a question!" he yelled.

"I, um, I have to use the bathroom."

"You gonna pee in the sink?" Two big hands grabbed her by the arms, dragged her across the room, and threw her down on the couch.

"Please?" Mia begged. "I just want to go home."

"Too bad. That's not happenin', least not yet. And quit your bawlin'."

He paced the floor to the window and back then grabbed and lifted her by the arms—his fingers digging into her flesh—and carried her down the short hallway and into the bathroom.

Mia stood petrified, not knowing what to do. Now she really did have to relieve herself, but how? With her wrists bound, there was no way to take care of what she needed to do. The last thing Mia wanted was to ask this man for favors, but she was completely at his mercy. Her eyes implored him to help her.

With a grunt, Benson reached into his pocket and pulled out a pocket knife. Mia gasped as he snatched her wrists and sliced through the zip ties.

When her hands were free, she waited for him to undo her ankles, but he slid the knife back into his pocket. The brute lifted her by the waist and stood her in front of the toilet, then turned his back and stood in the doorway.

Mia felt the heat rising in her cheeks as she finally pulled down her panties and gingerly lowered herself to the toilet. In that moment, for the first time in her life, she knew hatred.

***

"Why are you doing this?" Mia stared at her captor's back. No answer.

He rooted around in the grocery bag and pulled out a bag of doughnuts. After shoving one down in two bites, Benson turned to face her.

She saw nothing but malice on his unshaved face, and she didn't think he was going to answer. She was right.

When he did finally speak, she couldn't believe her ears. Or her eyes. "Time to get in your new house," he said.

Mia looked where he pointed. There in the corner was a really large dog crate, big enough for a St. Bernard or Great Dane—but certainly not for a person. Not even a small person like Mia. Her jaw dropped. He couldn't be serious.

She drew back when he reached for her, but there was no way to escape. Benson lifted her easily, carried her across the room, and set her down—hard—onto the dog bed in the crate.

"No, you can't put me in a cage!" Mia shouted, but Benson just laughed. Not a laugh of genuine humor, but a laugh filled with cruelty.

Once again, he pulled the knife from his pocket. He slashed the zip ties off her wrists and ankles, tossed the bag of doughnuts in the crate, and slammed it shut.

"Why are you doing this to me?" Tears streamed down Mia's face, but Benson simply turned and walked to the door. "Where are you going? You can't leave me like this." Mia's voice was shrill as she shouted, "I'm not an animal!"

Benson opened the door to leave but turned back and looked at his prisoner. With a grunt he trudged down the hall and disappeared into the bedroom.

Mia's mind raced. She opened her mouth to yell after him— she wanted to scream at his callousness—but fear choked out any words. *What is he going to do?*

Seconds later he returned, arms full, and opened the lock he'd placed on her chamber. Benson tossed a blanket and pillow in Mia's face and slammed the crate door again.

"Now quit your whining. I haven't done anything to hurt you, and I won't... unless you ask for it." He then lowered his voice and added, "Now. Shut. Up."

Mia drew back as far as her cage would allow and clenched the pillow in front of her. His final words and ugly laugh as he went out the door made her blood run cold. *Oh God, he's crazy.* What he said made no sense. She stared out the window at the brightening sky. *It's Saturday morning.* Mia thought about her parents, her brothers and sisters. She wondered what they must be thinking. Wondered if they were looking for her. *They must be.*

She replayed the man, Benson's, words in her head. What did they mean?

"You don't matter. You don't matter at all. You're just a little ole worm on my hook."

CHAPTER NINETEEN – SUSAN

Susan watched the sky lighten and knew the sun would soon give its Saturday morning greeting, but she wasn't ready for it. The night hadn't turned out anything like she'd thought. She was supposed to be waking in Marty's arms. Like turning back the clock. Everything would be exactly how it had been when they first married. Perfect.

But was it perfect, really?

Well last night certainly wasn't.

Susan looked down at her daughter finally sleeping peacefully next to her. This isn't the bed Susan had anticipated spending the night in, but plans change. Especially when your child needs you.

Elizabeth's sudden call for her parents to 'come quick' had been the beginning of a night full of perplexity. The child was totally distraught, and no matter how her parents had reasoned with her, she could not be convinced she hadn't seen 'that ugly man' on TV.

"It was him, Momma. It was just like in the dream." The child's chin quivered. "And he had that girl in a cage."

Pulling Elizabeth close, Susan looked up at Marty apologetically, and mouthed the words, *"Not now."* They had planned to tell their daughter of their plans to get back together, but she realized that must go on the back burner.

It had taken nearly an hour to calm Elizabeth and get her ready for bed. She'd clung to her mother and begged her not to leave. Of course, Susan had not planned to go back to her house on this special night. But neither had she planned to spend it curled up next to her little one.

Now she watched Elizabeth sleep, relieved that she had stopped tossing and turning with the night's recurring dream.

The child had awakened three times—each time more distressed—and been restless while sleeping. Marty had looked in on them a few more times and urged Susan to leave Elizabeth and come to bed with him, but she wouldn't budge. By midnight he had finally given up.

Susan knew he was frustrated, and she wanted to be with him. Yet she could not pull herself away from her daughter's side. Elizabeth needed her. Needed her more than Marty did.

Though she hadn't slept much herself, Susan quietly slid out from under the little bit of covers she'd held onto, stretched, and rubbed her cramped muscles. She pulled the lightweight blanket over Elizabeth, and, content that her baby girl was finally sleeping peacefully, crept from the room.

By the time she freshened up and made her way to the kitchen, she found Marty filling two mugs with freshly brewed coffee. The smell welcomed her into the room and into Marty's arms.

"I'm sorry about last night." Susan looked up into his eyes searching for his understanding.

"No worries." His smile lifted her mood as she accepted the steaming mug of coffee. He brushed the blonde locks off her forehead. "Did you get any sleep?"

"A little, but I can't say I feel rested," she admitted. "Elizabeth finally seems to be sound asleep. I'm worried about her, Marty. Why is she so obsessed with this idea of some ugly man hurting a girl? Do you think someone has scared her?"

"No, I think she would have told one of us if something like that happened, don't you? Lizzy usually tells us everything." Marty set his mug on the counter and took Susan's hand. "Now, let's talk about us."

"What about us?" Susan asked mischievously.

Taking the cup from Susan and setting it down, he took her in his arms. "Well, you said Lizzy is sleeping now, so..." As he tried to lead her from the kitchen, he felt her resist. "What?"

"I don't know. I mean, it just doesn't feel right." Susan glanced over her shoulder half expecting to see her child watching them.

There was no one watching, but still, it didn't seem like the right time. "Not now."

Marty heaved a sigh of disappointment and turned away. "Do you want something to eat?"

"No, just coffee."

"But you always had a big breakfast on Saturdays." Marty seemed suspicious. "Why don't you want anything?"

"I don't eat like I used to." Susan remembered those enormous breakfasts and how she had stuffed herself before going to the bathroom and purging. But through AA she had learned to manage her eating disorder along with her alcoholism. Now she began to sense how little Marty knew about the new Susan.

Her thoughts were interrupted by cries from Elizabeth's bedroom.

She found her daughter sitting up in bed wide-eyed, clutching her blanket. The child had yelled, "No, no!" Now tears streamed down her face. Susan ran to her side with Marty following close behind her.

Susan pulled her close whispering, "It's okay, baby, it's okay. Momma's here."

Marty stooped down by the bed and rubbed the child's back. "What is it, Lizzy? What's wrong?"

Elizabeth pulled back and looked at her mother with eyes wide. "It's Mia. Momma, he has Mia!"

Chapter Twenty – Val

"Andy," Val followed her husband into the family room, coffee in hand, "are you going to mow this morning? There's a chance of rain later today."

"Yeah, that's the plan. And why does it have to rain every Saturday?" Andy slumped in his chair. "We already cancelled this afternoon's round of golf. We'll try again tomorrow," he said rolling his eyes.

Val knew how he felt. She had hoped to do a little gardening in the afternoon, but it would have to wait for another day. She had the morning earmarked for finishing her latest article. Deadlines don't wait.

Bending over, she kissed her husband's cheek and headed to her office. "Well, we need the rain, yanno, to keep that grass growing for ya."

Andy tried to swat her on the butt for the snide remark, but she was too quick for him.

"Take it easy out there," Val called over her shoulder. Watching Bonnie go through the agony of losing her husband, Val had become more fearful of losing her own husband too soon.

"Don't worry," Andy chuckled, "that's also part of the plan."

It didn't take long for Val to be completely engrossed in the last bit of research she needed to complete her latest article, so she was startled when Andy appeared at her door just fifteen minutes later. "You can't be finished already," she teased. But seeing the expression on her husband's face, she added, "What's wrong?"

"I'm not sure. Craig just called." The crease between his brows deepened. "He's worried about Mia."

"What? Why? What happened?"

"I don't know if anything happened really. I mean she didn't come home last night. She just texted Sarah that she was spending the night with a friend, then turned her phone off."

"What? You mean she hadn't asked permission first?"

"No. I know it's odd, but kids do stuff like that, right?" Andy looked at her hopefully.

"Maybe some kids, but that's sure not like Mia. At least not that I've ever heard." Val felt her eyes being drawn to Mia's drawing still hung on her office wall. Looking at the cabin, she felt a chill. "Did Craig or Sarah call her friend's house?"

"They don't know who it was. She didn't say what friend." Andy walked to the window and stared out. "He said they're going to start making a few calls if she hasn't checked in or at least turned her phone on by lunchtime."

"I don't like it. I know Mia, and this isn't like her."

"Do you think this other girl might be influencing Mia?"

"Maybe, Andy. But as a rule, our granddaughter isn't that easily influenced." Val shook her head.

Andy took his cell phone out of his pocket, looked at the caller ID, and answered, "Susan. What's up?"

Val's eyes widened. Why would Susan be calling her husband? Then her heart quickened, thinking of Betsy. *Has something happened to Andy's daughter?* Listening to his end of the conversation didn't do much to answer the questions on her mind, but his responses made it obvious there was no emergency.

"That was weird," he said sliding the phone back in his pocket. Val saw the uncertainty deepen the lines in his forehead.

"What did she want?" she said hoping her irritation didn't shade her tone. But her annoyance faded as Andy relayed what was going on with Betsy. As much as she hated her husband's involvement with the *other woman's* child, she understood Andy's ties to his daughter.

Val pushed away the memory of how Betsy came to be born so she could focus on her present needs. After all, acting as her foster mother for months, she had learned to love Betsy, too.

"Does Susan have any idea why Betsy's having nightmares... or when they started?"

"Yeah, well sort of. Betsy told her and Marty about them one night when they were putting her to bed."

"Wait... what? Are they together again?" Val knew Marty had gotten closer to his ex-wife since Susan had been in recovery, and Val had hoped this day might come, but it was a shock to hear it might have actually happened.

"No, I mean Susan said he was there for dinner last Friday and stayed to tuck her in. When Marty told her to have sweet dreams, Betsy said she didn't want to dream. She said her dreams were too scary." Though Andy and Val typically referred to the child as Elizabeth when talking to Susan, they still thought of her by the nickname she'd chosen while living with them. "Here's the thing though, Val," Andy said moving closer. "Susan wants to bring her over here."

"Why?" Although Val loved the little girl, she wasn't anxious to have Betsy's mother in their house... with Andy.

"It's something about a picture. Apparently, Betsy is upset and insisting she has to show her parents the house." Andy shook his head. "Makes no sense to me. What house?"

Val knew exactly the picture the child was talking about. She remembered Betsy's reaction when she'd first seen it. The frightened child had turned and pointed to Mia's drawing. "That's the picture. I'm sure of it. But why?" she asked with an eerie sense of foreboding.

CHAPTER TWENTY-ONE – SARAH

With Destiny asleep on her shoulder, Sarah breathed in the sweet fragrance of baby shampoo, powder, and whatever other ingredients created the unique scent that warmed every woman's heart. It had a calming effect. But laying the sleeping baby down for her afternoon nap, it all came rushing back. All the anxiety and fear threatened to strangle her, but she fought to push them away. Right now, it was important to remain calm... for Craig.

With each phone call and each 'No, she's not here,' Sarah had seen her husband grow more alarmed.

Mia, where are you?

After calling a few of Mia's closest friends, Craig had called Shana, his colleague and Mia's art teacher, to see if she knew who his daughter had left with the day before. Sarah had seen the shock and disbelief on her husband's face when Shana explained there had been no after-school art tutoring by Mia—at least not that she knew of—and she was positive no one had used the art room following the final class of the day because she'd been there until four-thirty cleaning up and prepping for Monday's lessons.

Sarah listened to Destiny's intermittent sucking noises—she loved her pacifier at naptime—took a deep breath and quietly closed the door behind her. She heard voices coming from the family room. Val and Andy. *Craig must have called them.*

Craig and his parents had gathered in the family room. When Sarah got there, she saw the puzzled look on her husband's face and looks of concern from her in-laws.

"What's up?" she asked. "Have you heard from Mia?"

"No. But Dad was just telling me about something really strange." Craig turned back to Andy. "Dad, tell Sarah what you just told me."

Andy repeated the description of Susan's phone call and the visit that had followed shortly after.

"When I tried to take Betsy and Susan into my office to look at the picture, Betsy cowered behind her mother," Val said. "Her eyes filled with tears and she whined pitifully."

"Yeah, she was so upset I told her to stay with me." Andy looked toward his wife before adding, "Betsy is still comfortable with me."

Sarah didn't miss the look her in-laws exchanged and wondered what that was all about. But what Andy said next made her forget all about any of those concerns.

"The picture Susan wanted to see was Mia's drawing. You know, the one of the cabin in the woods?"

Sarah nodded dumbly in response. When she made eye contact with Val, Sarah saw a knowing look cross her mother-in-law's face.

"Sarah, angel, are you okay?" Craig had flown across the room and taken her by the shoulders. "What is it?"

"It's... it's that picture. I mean there's something about it." Sarah knew her words would make no sense, but she couldn't explain. It was her imagination. She was sure of it.

"Sarah," Val was standing next to her son now. "Something about that picture bothers you. I remember how you reacted the day you first showed it to me. What is it, hon?"

"It's nothing really," Sarah lied. "But why did Susan want to see it? I mean, I don't know why we're talking about some drawing when we've got something a little more serious to worry about." She could hear her voice getting higher and struggled to maintain control. "For God's sake, where is she?"

Craig pulled his wife into his arms as the tears Sarah could no longer hold back streamed down her face. "I don't know, angel," he said, "but I'm sure she's going to come charging through that door any minute." His voice choked as he tried to laugh. "And there will be some completely logical explanation. We'll all be laughing about this later."

Sarah looked up into her husband's eyes and read the lie in his words. *No. He doesn't believe that either.*

Andy, who had been sitting quietly for a while, spoke up at last. "Sarah, Craig, can you come sit down, please?" They did as he asked. "I know finding Mia is all that matters right now, but I think what I have to tell you could be relevant... and important. Or maybe it's nothing." Andy shrugged.

"What is it, Dad?" Craig sat on the edge of the couch still holding onto his wife.

"Like I said, probably nothing, but you know how close Betsy and Mia were when Betsy was living with us? And I think they still are. Mia's like a little mother with Bets." Andy took a deep breath. "Well Betsy has been having dreams. Scary dreams."

Sarah wondered what he was getting at. *What does this have to do with anything?* She leaned closer and watched her father-in-law intently, sensing the importance of this moment.

"She keeps talking about a scary, ugly man in her nightmares." Andy paused and looked over at Val who nodded her encouragement. "Betsy said this scary man has a girl—a girl who's trying to get away—and he's at the cabin that's in the picture."

Sarah gasped, and, wide-eyed, searched Andy's face. He had stopped talking again, and Sarah felt Craig's fingers digging into her arm.

"She is adamant. That's the cabin in her dreams. And there's more. Last night she said she saw the girl." Andy took another big breath, blew it out slowly and added, "She said it was Mia." Then he went on quickly. "But Sarah, you and I both know the dream probably doesn't mean anything."

Sarah interrupted. "No. No! It means something. I know it does. He has her. Oh God, Craig... he has her!" Her heart pounded in her chest.

Time seemed to stand still as four people sat frozen in silence. A chill filled the room, and Sarah wanted to scream, but she sat paralyzed, afraid to fully face the reality that threatened to destroy them all.

Sarah jumped at the sound of her phone. It signaled a text message. It was Craig who first moved. He dove for the coffee table where her phone showed one text, and automatically handed it to Sarah. With shaky fingers, she opened the message then her eyes went from Craig to Andy to Val. She saw the question and the fear in their eyes.

Turning back to Craig she whispered, "This can't be happening."

Craig took the phone from her and read the message out loud. "Sorry, but I'm not coming home." He shook his head. "I don't understand."

Sarah saw her own bewilderment mirrored in his eyes before he hit the favorites and tried calling his daughter.

"It went straight to voicemail," he said. Craig stood and walked to the window. With his back to the others he muttered, "This doesn't make sense." He spun around and gazed at his wife. She saw the bewilderment turn to alarm. "Mia isn't like that. My daughter wouldn't just say she's not coming home... would she?"

"No," Sarah murmured, "I don't believe Mia sent that text. I'm afraid Betsy was right." Sarah couldn't control the shaking that traveled through her body into her voice. "Our daughter's been kidnapped."

CHAPTER TWENTY-TWO – MIA

Overcome by nausea, Mia pushed the doughnuts away. She hadn't had any real food since lunchtime yesterday, so to answer the growling and spasming of her stomach, she'd finally succumbed to the sickening sweet temptation. Doughnuts. How many had she eaten? She pulled the box back and counted then groaned.

There had been ten when her captor tossed the box into the crate, and now she counted only six. *No wonder I feel sick.*

Her parents had nothing against sweets—in moderation. She couldn't remember ever eating more than two doughnuts in one sitting. She took several deep breaths trying to fight the rising queasiness. *Water. I need something to drink.* "I'm so thirsty," she said to no one at all.

Mia was completely alone... in a cabin... in a crate... somewhere in the woods. Like a caged animal. After Benson left that morning, she had screamed and cried until her throat hurt and her eyes burned. It was no use. Completely exhausted, her spirit crushed, she curled up with the pillow and blanket he'd thrown in the crate before he left. She realized she must have finally slept again when she was startled awake by the sound of tires. A door slammed. *He's back.*

Mia was at once relieved and terrified. The idea of being left there—locked up and alone—was frightening, but so was the idea of him being there and what he might have planned for her.

She rubbed her back and stretched her arms and legs, but she was still cramped. If she couldn't stand up soon, she thought she'd scream. *Maybe he'll let me out. Maybe he'll let me go...*

The door burst open and Benson walked to the cage and peered in. "Good girl. I see you ate your breakfast." He chuckled— it was an ugly, crazy laugh—and he turned his back on her.

"I'm thirsty." Mia's words were hardly more than a whisper.

Benson swung back around. "What? What are you mumbling about?"

"I... I said I'm thirsty."

Benson didn't respond but headed to the kitchen.

Seeing that he was getting her a glass of water, Mia screwed up her courage and ventured another request. "And I have to use the bathroom," she called to him.

When he finally unlocked the crate, Mia crawled out then stood and stretched.

"Well, go on!" he yelled.

Mia jumped and hurried toward the bathroom. At the door she turned and looked up at her captor. "Why are you doing this?"

Instead of giving her an answer, he gave her a shove into the bathroom. He took his usual station just outside the door until she was finished. When he directed her back to the crate, she hesitated.

"Please, don't make me get back in there. Can't I just sit on the sofa? I won't try to get away... I promise."

He lifted his chin in the direction of the couch and Mia quickly situated herself on one end. Benson rattled around in the kitchen, and though curious, she hesitated to look around to see what he was doing. Making eye contact might be a mistake.

Moments later she heard him coming toward her. He tossed something on the end table next to where she was sitting. The smell of peanut butter wafted up her nostrils and triggered her salivary glands. She snuck a quick glance at Benson, then at the sandwich.

"Well, go ahead and eat," he muttered.

Mia grabbed the sandwich, and it wasn't until she'd taken a huge bite that she wondered... *Did he drug this like he did that water?*

She didn't taste anything but peanut butter. He had put a generous amount of the sticky substance between two slices of white bread—not the good bread she was used to having at home—

and with no jelly or jam, her mouth got gummed up. Mia snuck a peek at Benson through her eyelashes and found him staring at her. Her skin crawled.

When he jumped out of his seat, Mia startled and nearly choked. But he charged past her into the kitchen and returned with two cans of soda. He slammed one down beside Mia, popped open the other one and took several gulps before plopping down again.

Deciding to try again, Mia asked, "Why won't you tell me why you brought me here? What are you going to do to me? I mean, you said you wouldn't hurt me, but..."

"That's what I said, and I meant it! Now drop it!"

"But..."

"I said, drop it!" Benson bellowed. "Now get back in there. Move!"

"No, please, I... I just—"

"You want me to tie you up again?" he threatened. Mia moved toward the crate. "You're lucky I gave you that blanket and pillow. Now quit complaining and get in."

Lucky? Yeah, right. Mia felt hopeless as she watched him head for the door.

"Don't worry. I'll be back. I'm not gonna let you starve."

"But I want to go home," Mia pleaded.

"Quit your whining. You'll go home when I'm done with you."

Benson slammed the door, and seconds later Mia heard an engine start up, tires spin and she was left alone again. She had no idea what time it was—lost without her phone—she searched as far as her spot on the floor would let her, but she didn't see a clock anywhere.

It had gotten darker out. Cloudy? Yes, she heard the rain hitting windows. A flash of light was followed immediately by the booming thunder. The sudden storm and darkness added to Mia's terror.

"Oh God, what have I done?" Mia slowly pulled herself to her knees, folded her hands, and did the only thing she could think to do. "Dear Lord, please help me. I'm sorry I got in the car with this man. I know I should have known better. But please help me. Amen."

Making herself as comfortable as she could, considering where she was, Mia tried to sleep. But then she thought of something else. "And Lord, please don't let my dad and mom be too worried... but help them to find me. Because I'm really scared."

And then she had another thought... or was it a voice that said, *"Trust in the Lord."*

"Thank you," she whispered. Pulling the blanket tightly around her, Mia listened to the rain—falling gently now—and finally, for the first time that day, she was at peace.

Chapter Twenty-three – Bonnie

The crease in Bonnie's forehead deepened as she said goodbye to Joe and hung up the phone. She hadn't wanted to cancel their plans for the afternoon, but it was obvious Val needed her. When she'd called a while earlier, her friend had said as much.

"Are you busy?" she had asked. Bonnie—who'd known Val since she first married Andy—recognized the quaver in her voice. Something was wrong. And nothing, not even Joe, could stand in the way of her being there for her friend.

"No dear, not at all," she had lied. *"Would you like to come over for some tea?"* Val's immediate positive response confirmed her suspicion. Yes, something was definitely wrong.

Since she was already brewing a pot of tea, Bonnie went to the kitchen and pulled out two of her favorite china teacups. She opened a tin of homemade oatmeal cookies, put several on a plate, carried them to the living room, and placed them on the coffee table.

Because Val had told her she was coming from Craig's house, Bonnie wasn't surprised to hear the car pull into the driveway so soon, but when she opened the door to greet her, she was shocked by Val's expression. "Oh dear, come in, child."

Val fell into her friend's arms.

"I don't know what it is, Val, but it's going to be all right."

"Is it? I'm not so sure." Val's eyes filled with tears.

"Come, sit down with me... we'll talk." Bonnie guided her to the sofa where Ginger promptly jumped in her lap and tried to shower her with kisses. "Not now, Ginger."

"It's okay, Bonnie," Val said putting her head down to accept the little dog's welcome. "Hello, s-s-sweet girl," she said, but her voice broke and whatever had been holding back the tears also broke.

Bonnie hadn't seen Valerie Reed this distraught since her marriage had nearly fallen apart.

"Val... dear, here," she said handing her a tissue. She waited until the tears subsided before speaking again. "Now, just breathe."

When Val gathered herself, Bonnie asked what was going on. She feared there might be a problem between Val and Andy. She was not prepared for what she heard.

"You think she may have actually been kidnapped?"

Val nodded.

"Okay child, you just sit here and keep breathing. I'm going to pour us some tea and we'll talk."

Back in the kitchen, when Bonnie reached to pour the tea, she discovered her own hands were shaking. Taking her own advice, she took several slow, deep breaths then poured. She carefully carried the tray with their tea into the living room, set it down, then took a seat next to her friend.

When Val finished telling her all she knew—including the details about Betsy's eerie dreams and Mia's drawing—Bonnie sat back against the sofa pillows. She absently petted Ginger, who was now cuddled on her lap, and looked intently at her dear friend.

"Val, I think we should pray for your granddaughter." It was a simple prayer: "Heavenly Father, we don't know where Mia is right now or who has her, but we ask that you watch over her and keep her safe from harm. And Lord, please comfort all those who love her and give them strength in this most difficult time. We put our trust in you. Amen."

***

By the time she left, Val appeared calmer and much more in control. Bonnie wished there was more she could do, but she felt completely helpless. Prayer was all she had to offer, yet she had promised to enlist the help of all her prayer warriors.

Phone in hand, Bonnie began the chain. She pulled out her list of the ten people she would call. Then each of them would make calls from their own lists. Bonnie had a mighty group of prayer warriors, and she had faith in the power of prayer.

When she'd thanked and said goodbye to the final person on her list, she had one more call to make.

"Hi. I know it's getting late, but do you want to go somewhere and get dinner? Or have you already made plans?"

"Don't be silly," Joe said at the other end of the line. "You're saving me from a can of soup and a ham sandwich. Where would you like to go?"

After a bit of discussion, they decided on carryout, so Joe picked up Chinese food and was at her door forty minutes later. Promising herself she'd get back on track tomorrow, Bonnie had thrown caution to the wind and ordered her favorite, Shrimp Egg Foo Young. Even Ginger was excited by the smell. She had to settle for her usual dog food but with a little dollop of the yummy brown sauce from her momma's dinner, she gobbled it up.

Before the humans sat down to eat, Bonnie laid out the good china place settings for two. And of course, there was a bowl for the rice—no eating out of cardboard boxes allowed here. Bonnie had reached that point in her life when she saw no need to save anything just for special occasions. Losing Frank after so many years of married life had thrown the fact of her own mortality sharply into focus. She would enjoy the things she had for as long as she had left. And then she would join Frank in paradise for all eternity.

But, for now, she was here on earth, and she was not alone. "I'm glad you hadn't made other plans, Joe." Bonnie served him the Orange Chicken he'd ordered as she added, "This is so much nicer than eating alone."

"Indeed." After saying grace, Joe picked up his fork, but before taking a bite he asked, "So what changed your mind? What's going on, Bonnie?"

Bonnie put down her fork and took a sip of tea. "I was just thinking. Life is short, right? And you never know..."

"That's true. But what brought this on?"

"A kidnapping, I'm afraid." As they ate, Bonnie filled him in on the little bit she knew about Mia's disappearance. "Joe, what are we doing?"

Joe's eyebrows shot up. "What do you mean?"

"Oh, I don't know. Never mind." Bonnie did know. But what she didn't know was how to approach the subject. "The shock of what's happened to my best friend's granddaughter must have me off kilter."

Joe shook his head. "It's a crazy world, sweetheart, but I'm sure she'll be all right."

"Thanks, Joe. It's hard to be so sure, but I'm trusting in the Lord." She hadn't missed what he said. Joe had never called her sweetheart before. *Hon*, yes, but not sweetheart. She kind of liked the sound of it. It fit. It felt comfortable. Yes, she liked it.

Since Joe insisted on helping to clean up when they were done, they made quick work of it. In no time at all the leftovers were in the fridge, and the few dishes were hand-washed, dried, and put away.

Bonnie poured them each another cup of tea, and they settled in the living room with Ginger comfortably sleeping between them. They chatted as they always did, yet there was an unspoken tension. Bonnie wondered if he felt it, too.

When it was time for him to leave, Joe put his hands on her shoulders, and she waited for the usual kiss goodnight. It had become customary. He would take her shoulders in his hands, pull her closer, and kiss her gently on the cheek. But when he pulled her closer, instead of kissing her cheek, he looked into her eyes. "May I?"

Bonnie felt the tension, and an excitement she hadn't felt in way too long. She simply smiled and nodded.

When his lips met hers, she knew she was ready. Yes, she was ready to be kissed... and so much more.

Chapter Twenty-four – Val

Val sat straight up in bed. She pushed away the blanket and threw her legs over the side. Though the window was open, and the cool night air had kept her under the blankets, now she was soaked with perspiration.

It was just a dream. But it seemed so real. Val got out of bed as quietly as she could and went into the master bathroom. She soaked a washcloth with cold water to wipe away the sweat of fear and tiptoed back to bed.

"What's wrong?" Andy pushed himself up on one elbow.

"Nothing really. I'm sorry I woke you." Val shivered and goosepimples covered her arms. She jumped under the covers and welcomed the warmth of her husband's body when he curled around her. "I just had a bad dream. It's no wonder, I guess."

"Mmm, yeah. I know. But try to go back to sleep." The groggy sound of his voice told Val he wasn't fully awake. And there was no sense trying to talk to him about the dream—or anything else—in the middle of the night. What good would it do? Besides, he was already breathing evenly with a slight purr at the end of each breath.

Andy's embrace, which had felt so warm and welcoming moments ago, had become a trap. Val now wished she could move without disturbing him, but it was too soon. She'd just have to be still until he returned to a deeper sleep. She thought maybe she'd even go back to sleep, too. Five minutes later she knew that wasn't going to happen.

Andy's breathing became deeper. His purrs became snores. Val carefully lifted the arm he had draped around her and slid to the far side of their king-sized bed. Though he stirred, Andy didn't awaken this time. He rolled away, probably thinking—if he was aware at all—that Val wanted him to roll over and stop snoring as she often did when the noise kept her awake.

But tonight, it wasn't Andy's snoring that made her lose sleep. *Five a.m.* Val got out of bed, grabbed her robe and crept out of the room. The memory of her disquieting dream followed her to the kitchen where she fixed a mug of coffee. This was promising to be a long and stressful day. She stared out into the darkness. *Mia, my sweet Mia, where are you?*

Like a nail to a magnet, Val was drawn to her office. Setting her coffee down, she looked at the drawing. *It doesn't make any sense.* Mia had given her this picture a week ago. *How?*

But Betsy was so sure. Val remembered the girl's reaction when she'd seen the picture hanging there. The child had been startled... and frightened. The dreams. She said that was the cabin from her dreams. At the time, Val assumed it was simply a child's imagination. But now?

Oh God, is Mia really in that cabin? Does he have her? Sarah had finally told them about the blue pickup she thought was following her and the eerie feeling she'd had when she saw the blue truck in Mia's drawing.

Val also wondered if there was something else Sarah wasn't telling them. Moving closer to the picture, Val peered into the truck. Were there people in there? Or was that just shading? No matter how much she squinted, she couldn't tell. Backing away, she shook her head. *I'm letting my imagination get away from me.*

***

Val wasn't sure, but the church appeared more jam-packed than usual this morning. Though she had considered not attending services today, Andy had reminded her there wasn't much more they could do for Mia besides pray—and what better place to pray than in God's house?

So, they had come early as usual, taken their seats in their usual pew, and then, when she'd looked around for Sarah and

Craig, she'd seen them in their usual spot as well. She also noticed how crowded it was. The sanctuary was often full, but this morning it was busting at the seams—sadly the kind of standing room only crowd typical only at Christmas and Easter services.

Val shot a questioning look at her son, but he shook his head. His eyes were evidence he probably hadn't slept well—if at all— and Sarah looked even worse. But they were here in spite of everything.

When Pastor Barns read from the old testament, Val thought she heard a sob from two rows back where Sarah and Craig were seated. He read from Isaiah 41:10: *"Fear not, for I am with you; Be not dismayed, for I am your God. I will strengthen you. Yes, I will help you, I will uphold you with my righteous right hand."*

Val understood. It was as though these words were being spoken directly to each of them. Then he read the Gospel of the day from John 14:27: *"Peace is what I leave with you; it is my own peace that I give you. I do not give it as the world does. Do not be worried and upset; do not be afraid."*

Andy squeezed her hand which she had to pull away to grab a tissue from her purse. *How can we not be worried? How can we stop being afraid?* Val blotted the tears that had suddenly snuck from her eyes, then placed her hand back in her husband's. When she glanced toward the choir, she saw that Bonnie was also dabbing at her eyes.

But they weren't alone. Apparently, this verse hit a lot of people. And why not? *This world has become such a scary place.*

Val marveled at the pastor's uncanny knack for giving them just what they needed. Then her lips curled up as she considered... *I guess he gets a little help with that.* Andy saw her little Mona Lisa smile and tilted his head and narrowed his eyes. "Tell you later," Val whispered.

When it came time for the sermon, Pastor Barns continued to preach to her family's need on this fear-filled Sunday morning. He opened with a passage from Philippians 4:6: *"Do not be anxious about anything, but in every situation, by prayer and petition, with thanksgiving, present your requests to God."*

Following the sermon, there was the usual altar call for those who had special prayers and Val and Andy were among the first on their knees. Bowing in prayer, Val felt a hand on her back as someone knelt on her other side. She looked into her son's red eyes before the closing words, and her heart broke a little more. Knowing she couldn't take away her child's pain drove her to deeper, more urgent pleas to God.

Please God, give my son the strength he needs and a way to get his daughter back. Please. And show me what I can do to help.

She usually ended her prayers with '*but thy will be done,*' but she couldn't utter those words even in her mind. Getting Mia back, safe and sound, was all that mattered. It simply had to be God's will.

When the service ended and the family all met on the parking lot, the hugs were longer and tighter than usual.

"Mom, I don't think we can make it for dinner this week. I'm sorry, but—"

"No, I understand. You have nothing to be sorry about. But what can we do? There must be something."

It was Sarah, while holding her youngest child, who answered. "Would you be able to watch the kids?"

Julie, Cody, and Bobby didn't know exactly what was going on, but they knew Mia hadn't come home. And their faces showed their understanding of the seriousness of the situation.

"We have an appointment with someone this afternoon," Craig added. "They're coming to the house."

"Yes, yes, of course. They can come with us now. Right, Andy?"

"Absolutely. Do you want us to stop by the house and get anything they need?"

"No, actually, we sort of knew you'd say yes," Sarah smiled sheepishly. "So I packed the diaper bag for Destiny, and they have what they need," she nodded toward the other children who headed for their car to gather books, iPads, and a couple of movies.

Bonnie had just come up behind them and embraced Sarah. "You're all in my prayers," she said softly, "and there are many more than you know who are also praying for Mia's swift return."

At that moment, Val knew why the church had been so crowded. "Your prayer warriors were here in force, weren't they?" she asked Bonnie.

"Many of them, yes," she answered.

"Thank you," everyone seemed to say in unison.

"You know what, Dad?" Craig said. "Why don't we follow you and drop the kids off instead of trying to fit this whole gang in your car and having to switch Dessie's car seat?"

"Aw, I wanna ride with Grandma," Cody said.

"Me too!" Bobby whined.

So it was decided, the boys rode with their grandparents while Julie and the baby followed in their parents' car.

"Grandma," Cody said, "do you know where Mia is?"

"No sweetie, I don't. But I'm sure she'll be home soon." It didn't feel like a lie. There was no reason to upset the children any more than they already were.

Instead of the usual chatter, the boys rode the rest of the way in silence.

And Val realized God had answered one of her prayers. At least now she had a way to help her son and daughter-in-law. She would care for the children, and she would continue to pray.

Chapter Twenty-five – Sarah

"This little one went sound asleep on the way over," Sarah said in a stage whisper. "Here, let me put her down before she wakes up. She should sleep for at least two hours if we don't disturb her."

Sarah got the baby settled in the same room Betsy had stayed in a year earlier. But now there was a crib. Sarah idly spun the mobile that hung above her baby girl, touching the white angel wings and clouds and the pink and gold hearts and stars.

She didn't know Val had followed her to the baby's room until the older woman put a hand on her shoulder and whispered, "Are you okay?"

Sarah put her hand on her mother-in-law's and nodded. "Thanks Val, I mean for watching the kids. I didn't think they should be there when we talk to the police." She turned to face Val. "I'm afraid it's just too much for them to handle. Cody and Julie are hardly talking at all—they just keep looking at us expectantly—and Bobby, who's trying to act like nothing's wrong, worries me even more."

"Well, right now you have enough to deal with. We'll take care of the kids while you and Craig do what you need to do to get our Mia back." Dessie stirred, and Val lowered her voice. "Shh, let's not wake her."

Val checked the baby monitor and silently followed Sarah out of the room. She almost ran over her daughter-in-law when Sarah stopped short.

"Val, do you mind if I take a minute to stop in your office?" She felt pulled to see Mia's drawing. When she did, it made her stomach churn, and she grabbed the edge of Val's desk, suddenly light-headed.

"Do you want to take it with you?" Val asked.

"Yes, I think I should... I'm afraid the police are going to think we're crazy, but I need to tell them everything."

Val put the picture in a big bag to take it out to the car. It was Julie who followed them out and asked, "What's in the bag?"

Sarah saw no sense in lying. "It's the drawing Mia gave Grandma." She saw the slight tilt of Julie's head, the frown that asked why, and a dawning of some knowledge of what it was all about. Julie was extremely perceptive for such a young girl.

"Mom, do you think she's okay?" Sarah saw her daughter's eyes glisten with tears as she spoke.

"Yes, Julie," Sarah answered with much more confidence than she felt. "There are so many people praying for her that I know she's going to be fine." She hugged her daughter tightly and released her so her father could do the same.

Craig gave her a big bear-hug, kissed the top of her head, and assured her Mia would be back with them soon.

***

"Craig, do you really believe what you told Julie?" Sarah had been staring out the windshield but turned to study her husband's face.

He reached over and put his hand on her knee. "Yes. I know it. She has to be okay. And she *has* to come home to us."

"Are we crazy? I mean it is just a drawing, and how could Mia have left us a clue even before anything happened?"

"No angel, I don't think we're crazy. None of it makes sense, but somehow... Do you think Mia had been to that cabin? That she remembered it?"

Sarah rubbed her forehead. "If she did, it must have been a subconscious memory because when I asked her about the drawing, she said it was just something she saw in her mind. Craig, I've suspected for a long time that your daughter has a gift. She sees things, you know, and draws them. And they mean something."

Craig didn't say anything immediately, and Sarah wondered if he did indeed think she'd lost her mind. Then he took a deep breath and glanced in her direction before looking back at the road. "*Our* daughter does have a gift. There's not a doubt in my mind. Whether the police will understand all of this is another question."

***

When Craig closed the door behind the detectives, Sarah fell into his arms. She could no longer control the tears she'd been holding back all day. "What are we going to do? They don't believe us. They think we're crazy. The one with the mustache wouldn't even look me in the eye."

"No, Detective Webb looked dubious, but I think the other detective—what was his name? Oh yeah, Evans—I think he was undecided. I mean he looked like he might believe it was possible."

"But what are we going to do? Craig, where is she? What if—"

"Stop it, Sarah," Craig interrupted. "Don't go there. We can't start imagining the worst. We have to have faith that Mia is all right."

Sarah gulped and tried to control her breathing. She knew her husband was right.

When she had gained control of her emotions, she asked Craig to call his parents and let them know they would come and pick up the children, and then went to the bathroom to freshen up.

By the time she returned, Craig was on the phone with his mom. He asked her to hold on and turned to Sarah. "Mom said the kids could spend the night there if we want. Do we want?"

"No. Tell her I appreciate it, but I really want the children here tonight. I *need* them here, okay?"

Craig smiled and nodded.

When he hung up, he said Val understood completely. "But she said for us to stay put. They're going to bring the children home to us."

Sarah sighed with relief. With Mia missing, she needed her other children. And later that night, when they were all safely in their own beds, she looked in on them one by one. Then she looked at Mia's empty bed.

Oh God, please bring our daughter home.

Chapter Twenty-six – Susan

Susan went to the front window and looked out. She was mystified by the phone call and why the police would want to talk to her.

"Momma, what's wrong?"

Susan turned to see Elizabeth staring up at her and holding her blanket. The child had only started carrying the blanket around again this week. Since the dreams. Since she'd seen Mia's picture. Since she'd become convinced Mia was in danger.

"Nothing's wrong, sweetie. I'm just watching for someone who's coming to ask me some questions." Susan didn't want to add to her daughter's anxiety by telling her too much. "Why don't you go play... or would you like to watch a movie?"

At Elizabeth's quick agreement, they started one of her favorites, *The Little Mermaid*, in her room. Susan hoped that would be enough of a distraction to protect her from anything disturbing the police might want to talk about.

And Elizabeth was settled just in time. Susan was about to check the window again when she heard a knock at the door.

The taller detective, who introduced himself as Detective Webb, filled the doorway with his presence. Susan almost didn't notice the other one, the one with the warm, brown eyes. But when she did see him, she sucked in her breath. Something about him drew her in. She was sure they'd never met, yet he was familiar.

"The Reeds say that your daughter seems to think some man has their daughter, Mia Reed." Det. Webb had pulled a notebook out of his pocket and was referring to notes he must have taken earlier. "Is that correct?" he asked.

Susan told him it was and filled him in on Elizabeth's dreams as well as the child's reaction to Mia's drawing. When she finished speaking, the second officer, who had introduced himself as Sergeant Evans, met her eyes.

He believes me. When their eyes met, she knew it. She wasn't so sure about Webb. The other policeman was professional, continued to take notes, and nodded a lot, but Susan could have sworn she saw him roll his eyes.

"Honestly Detective Webb, I think she somehow sees things, knows things, that we just can't understand."

Again, he nodded and wrote. "Sure, okay." Both his words and his sigh seemed to indicate he was simply indulging her. "Is your daughter here? Can we talk to her?"

Susan's chest tightened. How would Elizabeth be affected by the police interrogating her? "Is that really necessary? I don't want to upset my child any more than she already is."

"I think we have everything we need for now," Sgt. Evans said.

Susan shot him a grateful look but didn't miss the sidelong glance Evans got from Webb.

"Yeah, okay, Mrs. Walters. We'll let you know if we have any other questions."

Webb stood to leave, but Evans smiled reassuringly. "If you think of anything else, or if Elizabeth says anything you think might be helpful, please give us a call."

Evans handed her a card with his information, and when his fingers touched hers, Susan felt a warmth as warm as those eyes. *Stop it, what's wrong with you?*

She closed the door behind the two officers and leaned against it. *But why does he look so familiar?* It wouldn't be until the next AA meeting that she'd make the connection.

Susan shook her head and went to join Elizabeth on the bed. She found the child totally absorbed in the movie, propped up on all her pillows, but clutching her security blanket in one arm and her mermaid doll in the other. She looked so tiny to her momma. So vulnerable.

Susan crawled in next to her child and wrapped her arms around her. Elizabeth grinned up at her and returned the embrace, then cuddled in to watch the rest of her movie.

Before long, though, Susan heard her even breathing, looked down, and saw her eyes were closed. Although there were chores that could be done, phone calls to be made, Susan chose to stay.

She knew moments like this wouldn't last forever. All too soon, little Elizabeth wouldn't be so little. Wouldn't want to cuddle with her momma.

As she sat there absently fiddling with her daughter's soft, red curls, her mind wandered to the events of the night before.

What happened to the weekend she thought she'd have... the one Marty had planned? They were starting over. They were going to tell Elizabeth they'd be a family again. And—as Marty said—it would be just like before. Before her drinking got out of control. Before everything fell apart. Before she destroyed three lives.

But Marty doesn't understand. It can never be exactly like it was... because I'm not the same person I was before. I've changed.

CHAPTER TWENTY-SEVEN – MIA

Mia scrunched around in the small space she had, trying to get comfortable. She couldn't believe she was spending a third night in her tiny prison. She punched the pillow and flipped it over again. When she reversed it, the dirty pillow felt cooler on her cheek... at least for a fleeting moment.

The cool air circulating from the fan Benson had set up in the corner barely reached her. Mia blotted the beads of perspiration gathering on her forehead and neck. *Soon I'll smell as bad as Benson.* She felt sick just thinking about when he'd come in to feed her another peanut butter sandwich earlier. He'd reeked of dirt and sweat and bad breath and she nearly gagged trying to eat something he'd touched.

Mia rolled to her other side and skootched closer to the edge of the crate nearest the fan. Her body ached from being cramped in this small space for hours on end. The sleeping bag her captor had tossed in last night helped a little. Sleeping on the floor with nothing but a blanket under her had left her hurting so badly, she'd begged for at least an air mattress, but this was apparently the best he could do. Or all he cared to do.

Benson kept saying he wasn't going to hurt her, so why was he keeping her prisoner? Mia couldn't understand why this was happening. She begged God to help her find a way out, but he didn't seem to be listening. This was the third night, and she still didn't see any escape.

Pain and fear turned into anger. *Why God?* Mia's fingernails dug into the palms of her hands. Then her anger turned into tears streaming down her face. In desperation she pulled herself to her knees, thankful that, even though there wasn't room to stand, at least there was enough to kneel.

At first, she couldn't think what to say, how to pray. Mia knelt there feeling unable. She'd prayed every night yet now her mind was blank. Then she remembered something her mother had said to her before she died so long ago.

Mia was just a little girl at the time, and was upset and angry with her little brother. Jenny—her biological mother—had said maybe she should pray about it, but Mia replied she didn't know how to say anything but grace before dinner and her 'now I lay me...' bedtime prayer. And at this moment, she remembered her mother's words as clearly as if they were being spoken to her now. *"Just talk to him, sweetie, like you would talk to me or Daddy. And He will hear you, I promise."*

Thank you, Momma. Mia sniffed, wiped her nose on her sleeve, and spoke to God.

"Dear Lord, I'm sorry I've been so angry and haven't trusted you, but I'm just so scared. I don't know what to do. I've been really stupid. I know I shouldn't have gotten in the car with this man, but I... I believed him. I thought my pictures were so good I was gonna be famous. I'm sorry I was so vain... and so dumb." Mia swiped the tears that spilled down her cheeks. "I know Mom and Daddy must be so worried. Please let them know I'm okay, and please help me to get out of here and go home. I just want to go home."

Running out of words, Mia sat back on her heels and just breathed... and listened.

"Do not fear, for I am with you. Do not be dismayed, for I am your God. I will strengthen you and help you."

The words were spoken in her head, but she knew it was the Lord speaking to her. With her faith renewed, the fear didn't instantly vanish, but a slow blanket of peace covered her and lulled her to sleep.

***

Far away, in the small town of Madison, Sarah stared at the ceiling. "Craig, are you asleep?" she whispered.

"No. I just keep thinking about Mia. Out there, somewhere. Who knows where she is or if she's ok-kay?"

Sarah heard his voice crack on the final words.

"Wherever she is, I'm sure she's all right," Sarah tried to reassure him. "She's got to be."

She rolled closer to her husband and let him gather her in his arms. She wanted to believe what she said was true, but doubt had followed her all day, especially when she remembered Det. Webb's attitude. She wondered if they'd been taken seriously. It was only Sgt. Evans' comforting smile that was any reassurance at all.

Then she saw Mia. Sarah knew it wasn't a dream. She was wide awake. But she saw their daughter kneeling in prayer.

"Craig," she said pushing herself up on one elbow, "Mia's all right."

"Yeah, I know, but..."

"No, Craig, I mean I know she's all right. I saw her!" She felt the doubt and saw the incredulity on her husband's face and hurried on. "Seriously, I was just lying here, worrying, and then I could see her. I couldn't tell where she was, but she was kneeling, she was praying, and there was light all around her." The lines of worry melted into a smile of peace. "Our little girl is alive and well and under God's protection."

Tears of relief rolled down her cheeks, and when she looked at Craig, she saw that he believed.

Then they fell asleep, not knowing when or how, but knowing for a certainty their daughter would be coming home.

CHAPTER TWENTY-EIGHT – SARAH

Sarah watched Cody come into the kitchen rubbing sleep from his eyes and take his usual spot for breakfast. "Do we really have to go to school?" he asked.

"Yes, Cody," Sarah replied. "There's no reason for you to stay home."

"Right!" he yelled. "No reason at all!" The sarcastic words dripped with disdain. "Except that I haven't seen my sister since Friday, we don't know where she is," his voice grew higher and louder, "and nobody's doing anything about it." He nearly screamed the final words in what Sarah could only consider hysteria.

He would have stormed out of the kitchen had he not been intercepted by his father who had heard him and come running. "Whoa, Cody. Calm down, boy," he said holding him tightly in a cocoon of comfort. "Shh, we understand, shhh." Sarah looked on, wishing there was something she could do, but felt helpless. "Now listen," Craig was saying, "yesterday while you were with your grandparents, we talked with the police."

He pulled his son tighter and kissed the top of his head. Sarah saw his eyes fill and rushed to put one hand on her husband's back while rubbing Cody's with the other.

"Cody, I'm not sure if you'll understand this, but your father and I got a message from God last night. We know Mia is going to be okay, and she'll be home again... soon."

"If God can bring her home, then why doesn't He do it now?" It wasn't so much a question as a condemnation. This time he managed to pull away from his father and storm off to his room.

Sarah wanted to follow—to console him—but Craig insisted on giving him a little time to cry it out first. Craig assured Sarah he should be the one to talk to him—when he calmed down—and Sarah agreed, knowing the bond they had.

"Cody's freaking out," Bobby said entering the kitchen with Julie right behind. "Just sayin'."

"We know," Craig said. "He's upset about Mia."

"Can't blame him for that," Julie chimed in. "I'm scared, too. Have you heard anything?"

Craig reminded her and Bobby it was okay to be afraid. "We're all worried and upset. But your mother and I are feeling a little better today."

Sarah explained the revelation she'd had the night before, and Julie seemed immediately reassured. Bobby, not so much.

"Don't worry, Bobby. Mia and God are like *this*," Julie said putting the first two fingers of her right hand tightly together. "He won't let anything bad happen to her."

Sarah wished she felt as confident about that as she had the night before, but fear and doubt crept into the corners of her mind. *What if I just imagined it because I wanted it so badly?*

***

Though Sarah had cancelled most of her clients, there were a few, one young woman in particular scheduled for her second session, that she felt compelled to see in spite of the chaos in her own life. Somehow, she knew this client needed her... and needed her now.

At the end of the session, Sarah wrote her notes and closed the patient's file. This was another woman suffering from verbal and occasional physical abuse at the hands of a man who supposedly loved her. "This is going to be an uphill battle," she said to herself. The young woman believed her live-in boyfriend really loved her and that he truly meant it each time he apologized.

"He promised he's going to change... and he'll never hit me again," the client said. "I shouldn't have yelled at him for staying out so late. I mean he's a man, and he needs time to relax after work."

"So, assuming that's true," Sarah asked, "do you think that excuses him smacking you around?"

"Well, no, but like I said, he felt real bad, and he promised he'll never do it again."

Yes, this was going to take a while. But for today Sarah was satisfied that by the end of the hour, the young woman had a plan in place. A plan for that moment when she felt she might be in real danger. Sarah could only hope that if faced with such a threat, she'd use it before it was too late.

But then she thought of Holly who had been just like that when she first started working with Sarah. And look how far she'd come. Holly had finally kicked her abuser to the curb, and, as a much stronger, independent woman, was moving on with her life.

Thinking of Holly gave Sarah an idea. She pulled her file, found the number and gave her a call. After several minutes of catching up—and being thrilled with how far her old client had come—Sarah got to the point.

Holly reported that she hadn't heard from her ex since he'd blamed her therapist for their relationship ending, and she'd warned Sarah of his anger toward her.

"This may seem like a strange question, but what kind of vehicle does Ben drive?"

"Last I knew, he was driving an old Ford pickup."

Sarah's chest tightened; she could hardly breathe. She finally choked out her final question. "Was it blue?" She knew even before Holly answered. Of course, it was.

After reassuring Holly that it was nothing important—yet knowing her former client didn't believe a word of it—she ended that call then phoned the police, hoping to speak to Sgt. Evans. She wasn't anxious to speak with the rather unresponsive Webb again.

She was in luck. "That's like the vehicle in your daughter's drawing, right?" he asked.

Sarah was relieved. He really had been paying attention.

"Okay, well I'm glad you called," he said. "I tried to get in touch with you, but your secretary said you were with a client, and your husband was in class so I was going to try again later."

Sarah realized she'd been so distracted she hadn't checked her messages. "What is it? Has something happened?" She heard the panic rising in her voice and tried to control her breathing. It was useless.

"No, ma'am. But I visited the school, interviewed a few of her friends and some of the teachers, you know, to see if anybody saw her after school Friday."

"And? Did they?" Sarah thought she'd scream if he didn't soon get to the point.

"Well, no ma'am, but there was a custodian, Mr. Harris, who said he's pretty sure he saw her get in a car with some man."

"Pretty sure?" She didn't want to believe it. Why would Sarah get in a car with a stranger? Or was it someone she knew? And was it... "Was it the blue pickup?"

"No, Mr. Harris said it was a real nice silver Mercedes."

Sarah didn't know whether to be relieved or more concerned.

"He said the girl was carrying a big art portfolio so we're pretty sure it was your daughter. Oh, and he remembered the license number, because he thought it was funny. We're getting ready to run the plates now. Say, can I call you back, ma'am?"

"Yes, of course, and please stop calling me ma'am. You make me feel like an old lady, and I bet I'm younger than you."

The Sergeant said, "Yes ma'am," laughed, apologized, and promised to get back to her as soon as he could with more information.

Sarah had just one more client scheduled. She looked at the time and called her secretary. "Would you please call my five o'clock client? Tell her I'm sorry but will have to reschedule her... family emergency."

Chapter Twenty-nine – Bonnie

The scent of her fresh-baked cinnamon rolls greeted Bonnie and Ginger when they returned from their walk. "Mmmm, nothing smells so good, does it, girl?" She reached for the Tupperware container on the counter and took out a couple of treats. "Here you go, Gingersnap. Yes, you love these, don't you?" She laughed as the little dog took her treat into her little bed, gobbled it down, and returned for another. "All right, one more... that's all for now. Maybe I'll share some of my treat with you later."

Bonnie enjoyed baking. And Frank had always enjoyed eating everything she made. After he died though, much of the joy had gone out of so many things she'd done for him, like cooking and baking. Looking at the delicately swirling cinnamon buns dripping with cream cheese frosting, she smiled. "I bet Joe will enjoy these." Ginger tilted her head and her momma laughed. "Yes, I know you will too, but not yet."

Bonnie heard Joe's car pull into the drive and pushed the Keurig down to brew his favorite dark roast. Her tea was already steeping and she had just finished setting the table.

"Oh boy, something smells sinfully delicious," Joe said as soon as he walked in the door. He inhaled deeply and smiled. "Smells like Cinnabon in here."

"Fresh out of the oven," Bonnie agreed. "Come... sit." She set the big mug of coffee on the table. "Black, just the way you like it, though God knows how you can drink it without cream and sugar or sweetener."

"Nope, good coffee doesn't need cream or sugar. But you could come here and give me a little sugar if you want."

Bonnie saw the wickedly teasing look in his eyes, and she chuckled. "Here, you'll get all the sugar you need with one of these," and she lifted one of the big cinnamon rolls onto his plate.

"Thank you, sweetheart."

There it is again. As soon as Bonnie had also served herself, Joe took a big bite.

"Oh my gosh, I haven't had fresh baked cinnamon buns since..."

"Yes, I know. Your wife was a wonderful baker, wasn't she?"

"Ah, she sure was. That's one of the things you two had in common. That and your good taste in men," he said with a wink.

Bonnie remembered the good times the four of them had enjoyed together. Playing golf, occasional bridge games, dinners... good times. "Yes, I know how to pick a good man," she said. "And you are one of the best. I really appreciate you taking me to the vigil this afternoon."

As soon as Mia's disappearance had become known, the students at her school had insisted on organizing a prayer vigil for her safe return. Bonnie was amazed by how quickly they had gotten the word out through social media and contacting the local news stations. And she had done her part by using the prayer chain to spread the word to many of their church members.

"Any excuse to spend time with you, my dear," Joe teased. "But seriously, you must know I want to be there for Mia and to support Sarah and Craig." He shook his head. "I can't imagine what they're going through."

***

When they arrived at the school, the parking lot was almost full, and throngs of people—young and old—were milling about everywhere so Joe insisted on dropping Bonnie off before looking for a place to park.

As she was getting out of the car, Bonnie asked, "How in the world will you find me?"

"Just find a spot near the flag pole, okay? And I'll find you."

Bonnie stationed herself as directed and anticipated a long wait, but Joe was back by her side much sooner than she'd expected. "Wow, that was quick. Did you find a close spot after all?"

"No, I'm way over by the street, but a young man was kind enough to give me a ride back in his pickup." Joe chuckled, "He should charge for his valet services. He said he's going back and forth bringing people over. Seems to be enjoying himself."

Bonnie smiled acknowledging the thoughtfulness of a kind stranger.

She looked at her watch and raised her voice to be heard over the crowd. "Should be starting any minute."

There was the sound of someone tapping a live microphone, and suddenly the clamor ebbed and was replaced with an almost eerie silence. The sounds of a throng of sports fans turned into the hush of a church congregation.

Bonnie looked in the direction from which the sound had come and saw why. There at the microphone stood Mia's parents, her sister, and her brothers. To one side, Bonnie saw her best friend—Mia's grandma, Val—with Andy by her side.

"Oh, Joe," Bonnie whispered, "they all look so lost... so broken."

Joe put his right arm around her shoulders and held her left hand in his. She leaned into him appreciating the support. She was tired of being alone. Ginger was a wonderful companion, of course, but now she wanted more. It felt good to have Joe by her side.

Standing together they listened as Craig spoke about Mia's disappearance and thanked everyone for being here and for their prayers. When he was finished, several of Mia's teachers spoke about her character and what a brilliant and delightful student she was.

After the teachers, came the most moving part of the prayer vigil. It was the students' turn. They talked about Mia as a friend. One girl had written a touching poem that brought tears to many eyes. There were several songs and more testimonials.

Bonnie was tired from standing and swayed in Joe's arms.

"Sweetheart, do you think we should go?" Joe asked. "You must be exhausted."

Bonnie nodded and turned to leave but stopped at the sound of the next speaker's voice. She turned back and looked up at the young woman she had mentored. The woman she'd watched become an excellent therapist and an even better wife and mother... to her own children and to her step-children, Cody and Mia.

CHAPTER THIRTY – SARAH

Trembling, Sarah looked over the sea of faces. She had considered this vigil an astonishing tribute to the daughter she felt honored to be raising. And at this moment she was haunted by the thought that she had let the child's biological mother down.

When Sarah married Craig, she had not only promised to love him, but also to love and care for his children, Cody and Mia. And she did truly love them even then. Now she stood before all these people filled with guilt for not doing a better job. *How could I let this happen?*

Craig squeezed her hand and led her to the microphone. The crowd suddenly became hushed. Sarah wondered at the enormity of the moment. How could so many people be so silent? The only things she could hear were her own breathing and the sound of her heart pounding in her chest. *What should I say?*

"Thank you all for coming out." Sarah couldn't control the quiver in her voice. She wanted to turn and run. Hide her shame. Put a pillow over her head. But she *needed* to be here. To do this. "And thank you for loving and caring about Mia. The last few days have been a nightmare," Sarah swallowed hard, "and we miss her so much."

She spotted Bonnie and Joe in the crowd. Saw her bridge club friend's smile of encouragement.

"If any of you know anything that might help us find her, please contact us or the police." Sarah's eyes moved through the crowd, looked at each face, and saw the same sort of sorrow, concern, love, on each one. They helped her to go on in spite of the cold sweat. "Most of the people we've talked to have asked if there's anything they can do. The best and most important thing you can do is pray."

Sarah had continued to scan the throng of people, but she suddenly saw something that didn't fit. Her eyes stopped on the face of one man among all those people. His face was wrong. He was smiling... No, *smirking*.

She forced herself to go on in spite of disquiet crawling up her spine. "Just before coming here, we talked to the police, and they do have a lead. Thanks to something someone saw, they have information on the car, and they're going to find the person who has our daughter."

Amid the stillness of the crowd, an abrupt movement caught Sarah's attention. It was the smirker side-stepping his way to the edge of the crowd.

Sarah knew that face. She sucked in her breath. "It's him," she whispered.

Despite the horror attacking every fiber of her being, no one else moved. There was complete, endless silence. Finally, startled by hands on her shoulders, her head snapped around to face her husband.

Craig's eyes widened. "What is it? What's wrong?"

Sarah couldn't speak. Couldn't find the words.

"Sarah?" Craig said, gently shaking her by the shoulders. "Are you all right?"

Finding her voice at last, she barely breathed the words, "It was him. I saw him."

"Who? Who did you see?"

"The man who took our daughter."

A murmur ran through the crowd growing louder and louder.

Val and Andy stepped forward. "What's happening?" Looking at Craig, Val asked, "Is Sarah okay?"

Mouth opened, Craig looked back at his mother, shook his head and shrugged.

It was Andy who took the mic, thanked all the people gathered, asked for their continued prayers, then handed it back to his friend, the art teacher who had helped organize the event. He whispered to her, "I think my daughter-in-law is overwhelmed. We'd better take her home."

Sarah stopped to quickly ask Pastor Barns to pray for Mia's safe return then allowed Craig to lead her away from the throng of people.

By the time they reached the section of the parking lot where they'd left the car, Bonnie was hurrying toward them. "What happened? Sarah dear, are you all right?"

Sarah felt all eyes on her and looked from face to face. It was time to tell them all her suspicions. "I think I know who took Mia." She turned and looked into her husband's eyes. "Craig, I'm sure of it. I saw him... just now... in the crowd."

The lines in Craig's forehead deepened as his brows lowered. "What are you talking about, Sarah? How could you know... I mean, we don't know who took her."

"Sweetheart, there's something I haven't told you." Sarah saw the confusion on her husband's face. When she looked from her in-laws to Bonnie and Joe, she saw Craig's expression mirrored on each of their faces. She took a deep breath. "Do you remember the blue pickup parked next to the cabin in Mia's picture?"

"Yes," Val said, "and it seemed to bother you. Why, Sarah?"

Sarah told them about her client's warning. She told them about the day she'd met the dark stare of a strange man with his straggly brown hair and an unkempt moustache. And she finally told them about the metallic blue pickup.

At first, she was met with blank stares. It was Val who first responded. "You think that's why Mia had the truck in her drawing?"

Sarah read the doubt on her mother-in-law's face. *She thinks I've lost it.*

But Bonnie, lips pursed, drew closer. "You hadn't told Mia anything about this man or the truck, right?" she asked. When Sarah shook her head, Bonnie added, "So you think this might be part of a message she had... from somewhere?"

Sarah couldn't find her voice. She could only nod in agreement. She had been focused on Bonnie, but when she turned to face her husband, she detected a change in him.

The hands that held her just moments before, now hung at his sides. "And now you think this mystery man was here? You saw him?" Craig asked.

Sarah nodded and wondered at the tightening in her throat.

"But how can you be so sure it was him and that he took her?" Andy asked.

"He smiled."

"What?" Craig asked incredulously.

Sarah turned back to face her husband again. "I know it sounds crazy, but you didn't see his face. I mean, it wasn't so much a smile as a sneer. It's like he was telling me something."

Craig took a step back, shook his head, and turned to face his parents. "Damn it, Sarah! Why haven't I heard any of this before?" Before she could attempt to answer, he went on, "I guess we'd better contact Det. Webb. I think this is information he needs to know." He walked around and hopped into the driver's seat while Sarah stood frozen by the side of the car.

"Don't worry, we've got the kids," Val called after her.

Bonnie put an arm around Sarah and whispered, "Go ahead, dear. Get in. Tell the police. I have a feeling your Mia will be home with you soon." She gave Sarah a reassuring squeeze and opened the car door for her.

Sarah slid in beside her husband and looked at his profile. The set of his jaw was unsettling. She put her hand on his knee. Normally his reaction to that movement would be to place his hand over hers.

But both hands remained firmly on the wheel. Craig pulled out of the parking spot staring straight ahead. Sarah saw the nerve in his temple throbbing... just like her heart.

Chapter Thirty-one – Mia

Mia scratched her head and pulled her fingers through her hair. Since she was in the habit of washing her hair daily, going three days without a shower added to the misery of her captivity. Her hair felt oily and dirty. She hadn't bathed since Friday morning and, no matter how awful she felt, couldn't possibly ask *him* if she could take a shower. *I feel so cruddy.*

She ran her tongue over her teeth. There was toothpaste in the bathroom—though she doubted Benson ever used it—but putting it on her finger and rubbing her teeth didn't leave them feeling clean. Maybe tonight he'd bring her the toothbrush she'd been asking for. Was that too much to ask? Mia tried to make the most of the situation in which she found herself, but why should she ask for things to make her new life more bearable here? Wouldn't that be like accepting that she was stuck here? That she'd never get away?

No! I will get out of here. Then she heard what she'd been listening for with anticipation and dread. She hoped this time he'd have something decent for her to eat. Mia wasn't used to a diet of nothing but doughnuts and peanut butter sandwiches. She craved a real dinner like her mom made. Maybe a nice pork chop or piece of chicken and some mashed potatoes. Yet now, with her stomach growling loudly and having only had one sandwich all day, she would have happily settled for anything.

Benson burst through the door and just stood there staring down at her. There was no bag of food in his hands. Mia thought perhaps he'd left it in the car, but why would he do that?

However, her worry about what he'd brought for dinner vanished when she saw the contorted expression on his face. His image filled her with dread. Benson's teeth were clenched and his hands balled into fists. *Oh God, don't let him hurt me.* Mia began to shake and pulled herself to the far corner of the crate.

And still he stood there silently seething. The only movement was in his eyes as they darted back and forth searching. Mia wanted him to move, to say something. Anything had to be better than this. At least that's what she thought... until it happened.

He took a step toward her. Then another. Then, without warning, he kicked the crate so hard it slid across the room and slammed into the wall. When she looked up, Mia saw him glaring at her and was mortified that she'd lost control of her bladder.

"Damn it!" he shouted.

Mia, already on her knees, prayed silently, *Lord, protect me. Please...* She realized Benson wasn't looking at her so much as through her. She didn't think he even saw her. Desperate to go to the bathroom, to clean up, to eat, Mia wanted to scream. But she was afraid to so much as whisper.

Benson turned and strode out of the room.

Where is he going?

She could hear him in the bedroom muttering to himself. His voice rose and fell so she could only catch a few words here and there. "...bitch..." "...her fault..." Mia heard him moving around. "...disappear now..."

Moments later he stomped down the hall and headed for the door.

"Mr. Benson," Mia's voice came out of fear and desperation. *He can't leave me here again.* She hadn't eaten for hours and still had to go to the bathroom.

He stopped, apparently startled by the sound of her voice, and turned to look back. His expression seemed to show he'd forgotten all about her. Maybe he'd let her out for a while now.

"Mr. Benson," she repeated more timidly, "can I please use the bathroom?"

"This is her fault, you know."

Mia had no idea what he meant. "What is? I mean who..."

"The whole thing," he growled. "It's all her fault. We would've been all right if she hadn't stuck her nose in and ruined everything."

None of this made any sense. *He's crazy.*

"Please, can you let me out for just a little while? Please?" She saw his agitation. She saw the duffle bag in his hand. *What's happening?*

"Gotta go," he said more to himself than Mia. "Gotta get away."

And then he was gone. The door slammed behind him. She heard a car door bang and the engine started. The wheels rolled down the dirt road, and Mia sat dumbfounded in the deadly stillness it left behind. Breaking the silence, her stomach growled noisily again, and her head ached.

She didn't know how long she sat immobilized, but in the end, she had to surrender to her bodily need to relieve herself. She pulled her sundress up around her waist, removed her panties, crawled to the far corner of her cage, and squatted. Her tears flowed as she watched the urine run across the floor, draining away her final bit of dignity.

CHAPTER THIRTY-TWO – SUSAN

Susan and Marty didn't talk much on the way back to pick up Elizabeth. Like every parent, they related Mia's kidnapping to how they would feel if their daughter were to disappear. Susan had lost Elizabeth once and remembered the pain of that separation. But she had known her daughter was safe in Andy and Val's care. She couldn't imagine not knowing if her child was dead or alive. The thought sent a shiver through her.

"Are you all right?" Marty asked.

"What?" Susan was pulled from her reverie. "Oh, yes. I was just thinking about poor Sarah and Craig. They must be going crazy, and Sarah looked ill when she left."

"They're going to find her, Suze... and she's gonna be okay."

Susan wanted to believe him but thought of all the times she'd heard of children disappearing only to have their lifeless bodies found days, weeks, or even months later. "I hope you're right, Marty. She's such a sweet girl, and Elizabeth adores her."

Mia had taken the younger girl under her wing in the months she'd spent living with Val and Andy, and Elizabeth had gone to her for comfort when she was hurting.

As soon as Marty parked the car in Susan's driveway, she hopped out and headed over to Amber's house next door. But before she even reached the front door, it sprang open and Elizabeth ran toward her. "Momma, me and Jordan watched *Happy Feet* again." It was one of her favorite movies.

"Did you pick that one, or did you let Jordan choose this time?" Susan asked.

"She picked it. Well, it was my idea," Elizabeth added with a sly grin, "but she said okay 'cuz she likes it, too."

Susan sent her daughter to Marty's waiting arms while she went in to thank Amber for letting Elizabeth spend the afternoon.

"No worries. You know Jordan loves it when she comes over," Amber said. "And I hope you don't mind, but it was getting kind of late, so I let them have supper awhile. Just chicken fingers and mac and cheese."

Susan thanked her neighbor again and headed back to her house where she found Marty sitting on the couch, book in hand, with his daughter cuddled up to him. Leaning against the door, she smiled with satisfaction. *This is how it should be.*

"Oh hey, Lizzy says she already ate so we're just hanging out."

Although her daughter would always be Elizabeth to her, Susan loved hearing Marty call her by the nickname he'd given his baby the first time he held her. *He is her father in every way that counts.*

***

"I guess I should go," Marty said, taking Susan's hands in his.

Elizabeth was settled for the night. He and Susan had shared a quick supper of homemade potato soup and tuna sandwiches though neither had much appetite. He leaned against the kitchen island and though Susan heard the words he spoke, she saw that his eyes said something else. *He doesn't want to go... and I don't want him to go.*

"No," she said, "stay."

"Are you sure?" he asked tilting his head to one side. "I'm kind of getting mixed messages here, Suze. I mean, I thought we were on the same page, but then... I don't know. Something changed. You seemed to change your mind."

"No, Marty. I haven't changed my mind," Susan said softly. "I just... I'm not totally sure you're aware of some things." She saw his confusion and felt him pull away as he dropped her hands.

"Like what? Is there something else you're not telling me? Something about Andy maybe?"

Susan's jaw dropped. "No! Oh my God, you can't think I..." She couldn't finish the thought. "It's nothing like that."

"Then what? What other secrets do you have?" Susan heard the edge in his voice, the lack of trust. "Well?" he asked.

"I don't have any secrets," she said louder than she intended. She was struck by the realization that he didn't trust her. And that hurt.

Hurt turning to anger she muttered, "Maybe you're right. Maybe you should go." Susan turned her back on the man she loved. She'd lost him once. Was she going to lose him again? *No, we just need to talk this through.* She knew she had to explain how she'd changed, that's all.

Susan turned to apologize, but as she did, the click of the door closing behind Marty told her it was too late.

Chapter Thirty-three – Sarah

Sarah sat, hands wrapped around her mug, breathing in the soothing scent of her first morning cup of hazelnut coffee. Hoping it would take away the chill she drank deeply, but, while it warmed her tongue and throat, it couldn't loose the icy fingers of foreboding.

She checked the time, knowing it was still too early to call Holly. But at least she could call her secretary who should be up getting ready to head to the office by now.

Sarah made the call to be certain any emergencies were given to her colleague, Brian, who had assured her he and the others could cover her caseload until Mia was safe at home again. Her father-in-law, Andy, was still seeing some of his own clients, but with him and Sarah both needing to take time away from the practice, it took a shared effort on the part of the other therapists to provide continued care for some of their neediest patients.

Before long, the children somberly trooped in for a breakfast of cold cereal. Sarah was struck by the difference in mood from their normal liveliness. She thought she should probably do something... say something, to lift their mood. But it was hopeless. How could she lift their spirits when hers were so low? She lacked the strength to even make an attempt at levity.

The children had each expressed their desire to stay home the night before, and Sarah remembered Cody's plea as being the most heart-wrenching. "How am I supposed to pay attention to stupid math and stuff when I don't know where my sister is?" He had swiped away the tears he couldn't hold back and cried, "She's my sister!"

"I know baby, I know."

Cody would normally have objected to being called 'baby' but he didn't seem to notice. Sarah had pulled him onto her lap and rocked him. He'd lost too much already in his short life. He'd lost his mother so young, and Sarah knew he was afraid he'd lost his sister now, too.

"But we're going to get your sister back, I promise," she said. And she prayed it was a promise she could keep.

Craig came into the kitchen shortly before the kids had to catch their bus—more sullen than any of the children—then poured himself a coffee and leaned against the counter without so much as a 'good morning' to his wife.

He and Sarah said goodbye to Julie, Cody, and Bobby before they went out the door. And they hugged them a little tighter and a little longer than usual. Sarah said a silent prayer that she'd get to hug their sister again... soon.

"Craig, are you all right?" she asked as soon as the door closed behind the last child.

"What do you think?" he said with cold sarcasm. Sarah shivered. "Did you call her yet?"

Before going to sleep the night before Sarah had promised she'd get in touch with Holly first thing in the morning.

"Not yet. I... I didn't want to call too early."

"Well, I think your client might forgive you for disturbing her sleep under the circumstances." The frostiness of his words and his expression cut into Sarah like an icicle stabbing her heart.

"I'll call now," she said nearly in a whisper, swallowing the knot in her throat. She turned to get her phone but hesitated, knowing she couldn't talk until she got better control of herself. Turning back to look at her husband she whispered, "I'm so sorry," and with the words came the tears.

She looked into her husband's eyes and saw the cold stare begin to melt. Then in an instant it dissolved into a loving look of forgiveness—or at least sympathy—and he took her in his arms. He held her so tightly it hurt, but she didn't pull away.

"It's all right, angel. I don't know why you didn't speak up about this guy sooner, but this is no time for us to snap at each other," Craig said hoarsely. "I'm just crazy with fear, but I'm not blaming you. I'm just trying to understand."

But you don't.

An hour and a half later they had dropped Destiny at daycare and were walking into the police station where Holly promised to meet them. She had heard about the missing child, and when she realized it was her therapist's daughter, she'd worried that her ex might be involved with the disappearance.

While they waited for Holly, Webb and Evans filled them in on what they'd learned about the vehicle Mia had gotten into Friday afternoon. They'd determined the silver Mercedes was rented under the name 'Benson' but not returned properly. One of their employees discovered it when he came to work Saturday morning. It was parked on the street, around the corner from the rental agency.

"They were pretty pissed at the condition of the car, too," Webb said. "It was dirty and smelled of liquor and sweat. That's when they discovered the information on the rental agreement had been falsified."

Holly hurried in just then and hugged her former therapist. "Sarah, I'm so, so sorry. I can't believe this is happening. And I'm sorry I couldn't get here sooner, but I got rid of all the pictures I had of Ben. I had to find one on my computer and send it to my slow printer."

Sarah, who would normally say something to help her client understand it wasn't her fault, could only focus on why they were there. Eyeing the folder Holly held under her arm, Sarah asked, "Is that the picture?"

Holly nodded and opened the folder. It held a wedding picture. There stood her client all dressed in white and a fairly good-looking, clean-shaven young man. But even without the straggly beard, Sarah saw what she needed to see. Though not as disheveled, she recognized his face.

"That's him," Sarah said. "That's the guy I saw in the pickup that day and in the crowd last night." She turned and looked up at her husband through a blur of tears. "He has our Mia."

Craig took the picture, handed it to Det. Webb—who'd been waiting with Evans and the FBI agent working on the case—and took his wife in his arms. "We'll find him, angel, and we'll find *our* Mia."

Carter, the FBI agent, pulled Holly aside and began questioning her about her ex-husband and anything she might know that could help. It was when he asked if she had any ideas as to where he might go, where he might hide, that Holly paused. She frowned for a moment then looked at Sarah, eyes wide.

"What is it?" Sarah asked.

"I... I'm not sure." Holly turned to agent Carter. "But his family had a cabin. I mean, he never uses it much because it holds a lot of bad memories... but sometimes—when he'd be in one of his moods—he'd go there." Sarah saw the pain on her client's face when she added, "He took me there once and threatened to put me in a cage and leave me there."

"A cage, you say?" Carter, who'd been jotting notes on a pad, stopped writing and wrinkled his brow.

Holly nodded, glancing over at Craig and Sarah. Sarah didn't miss the tortured look on her face and was torn between wanting to comfort her client and, more urgently, wanting to find her daughter.

Holly went on to explain that Ben's father, Ben Sr., had been a cruel and abusive drunk. He had often locked his son in that enclosure with nothing to eat or drink for hours or days at a time.

"Holly," Sarah was scrolling through the pictures on her phone frantically, "does the cabin look anything like this?"

She showed Holly the picture of Mia's drawing. Holly looked stunned as she nodded.

"Let's see that," Carter said. "So, you've been to this cabin, Mrs. Reed?"

Sarah read the confusion—and was it suspicion—on the agent's face.

"No," she said quickly, "our daughter, Mia, drew this."

Carter, who had been sitting on the corner of Det. Webb's desk, stood up and took a step toward her. "So, she knows this man then?"

"No!" Sarah knew he wasn't going to understand but rushed to explain. It was Evans who surprised her.

"Agent Carter, it would seem that the child has a gift. She draws things that she's inspired to draw," he said. "The parents told us about this drawing, but we didn't know if it was relevant."

Det. Webb was nodding agreement, but Sarah could see the FBI agent was skeptical.

"Okay people," Carter said putting the notepad away. "We'll get to the bottom of this. We don't know for sure that she's with this guy, but right now I guess we need to find this cabin." He turned to Holly. "Mrs. Garfield, where is it?"

"I... I'm not sure exactly. I was only there that one time, but I know it's the other side of Johnstown. I think I might be able to find it."

"Okay, you're coming with us." Carter, who had obviously taken charge, decided Sarah and Craig would come with them, explaining they'd be needed for identification.

Sarah figured he must have seen the look of horror on her face because he quickly went on to clarify that neither he nor the detectives had ever met Mia and wouldn't recognize the child. "Plus, if Mia's there, she may be frightened after her ordeal. It will be good for her to see you."

Holly looked at Sarah. "I'll find it, Sarah, I promise."

But will you find it in time?

"Sarah, let's go." Craig turned and hurried out of the station ahead of her. He glanced back once and called, "Hurry Sarah! We've wasted enough time." The gentle comforting tone of moments ago was gone, replaced by that earlier tone... the one filled with agitation and blame.

Chapter Thirty-Four – Mia

Mia opened her eyes, but saw nothing. Engulfed in blackness, she sat as still as the night. She wondered if Benson had returned while she slept. She sat up and listened. Nothing. Not a sound. On the previous nights, each time she'd awakened, she'd heard Benson snoring and moving around restlessly. But tonight nothing. *He didn't come back...*

Choked with fear, Mia began to shake uncontrollably. She pulled the blanket tightly around her and cowered in the corner. *What am I going to do?*

"Father in heaven, what am I going to do?" she sobbed. Knowing she was alone, Mia let her fear and frustration escape in a primal scream. She screamed and screamed until she was hoarse. And then her crying turned to laughter. "Now I know I'm alone... and I'm talking to myself. God, help me, I'm going to lose my mind." Her thoughts jumped in every direction considering all the things that might happen. And none of them were good.

"You're going to be okay."

Mia didn't know where the thought came from, but it was loud and clear. And she wanted to believe it. *But how?*

Her eyes searched the room. She looked at the lock on the crate. On her knees she shook the crate like a prisoner shaking the bars of his cell... and had just as much luck. She sank back on her heels. Defeated. *If he never comes back, I could starve... I could die here.*

"HELP! SOMEBODY HELP ME!" But Mia remembered the trail to this cabin. They hadn't passed another dwelling for miles. No one was going to hear her. She was on her own. Doomed.

"Daddy," she cried, "Please help me." Her words ended in a sob of desperation.

147

Find a way! It seemed an unpromising idea, but the thought persisted. *Find a way!*

Again, Mia scanned the room, but this time her eyes stopped on an object she hadn't seen before. There on the end table next to an overstuffed chair. A key. There it was, her only means of escape. Right there in plain view... but completely out of reach.

Those few seconds of hope drove Mia into even deeper despair. In utter frustration, she threw herself onto the floor. But when she did she noticed something. The crate moved. Not much, of course, but it definitely moved a few centimeters. *This is the way.*

So, Mia tried to push the crate again. Nothing. Again. Nothing. Tears flowed as she tried once more—without budging—before collapsing to the floor.

Mia realized with exhaustion she must have slept again because when she roused next, the room was lighter. The sun was just beginning its daily journey, just as she knew she must begin hers.

With new determination, Mia threw herself against the end of the crate. *Yes! It moved.* She repeated her effort again and again. At first, she only felt movement every fourth or fifth time and her progress was barely noticeable. She wanted to give up many times but knew she couldn't.

After what seemed to Mia to have been hundreds—or thousands—of attempts, and pushing through the pain of repeatedly banging her small body against the metal cage, she found herself close enough to reach the table. Turning her hand sideways she slid it through one of the openings in the crate. Even though she was slender, she couldn't get more than her hand through the opening. *No!* Just out of reach.

Mia let out a screech and threw herself against the enclosure one more time. It hit the table, and the key was jostled from its resting place to the very edge of the end table.

Mia wiped her sweaty hands on her dress and anxiously slid her hand toward the key once more. When her fingers touched the metal, she sucked in her breath and held it. She was able to turn her hand just enough to grip the key between two fingers and gingerly bring it back through.

Finally, with the key to her freedom clasped firmly between folded hands, Mia gave thanks to God.

***

It had taken several attempts before Mia was able to at long last open the lock and crawl out of the crate. Her young body ached, and she knew she'd have lots of bruises from her ordeal, but she was out. Her legs were a bit shaky but they carried her to the door. Pulling it open wide, she sucked in the cool, fresh air. After living with the stale smell of urine, Mia wanted nothing more than to use the bathroom and wash up.

That done, she went to the kitchen in search of something to eat. All she found was one stale doughnut and a couple bottles of water. She wolfed down the doughnut and one of the bottles of water before heading back outside. Benson could come back— though she doubted he would—and she didn't plan on being there if and when he returned. She looked down the road.

How far had they driven after seeing the last cabin? And would anybody even be there? *If only I had my phone.* Benson had taken it, but what had he done with it? *Maybe...*

She hurried back inside and searched feverishly. It was nowhere to be found. Having rummaged through the meagerly furnished bedroom, Mia stood looking at the bed in utter weariness. "Just for a minute," she whispered. She sank onto the bed, drew her legs up, and the now unfamiliar comfort almost instantly lulled her to sleep.

And in her sleep, Mia dreamed. She dreamed of being home with her mom and dad. She dreamed of laughing with Julie and bickering with Cody and Bobby. And—with the fatigue of the ordeal Mia had endured for the last four days—she sank into a deep sleep that went on for hours. She slept until she was jolted awake by the sound of an approaching vehicle.

Chapter Thirty-five – Bonnie

Bonnie got up from her knees and walked to the window. She didn't usually kneel to pray—didn't think God cared what position we were in when we speak to him—but her fervent desire to reach Him now had driven her to her knees.

"Please God," she had prayed, *"keep her safe. Protect her and let her be unharmed. Guide whoever has her to let her go and bring her safely home to those who love her. Oh please, I beseech you, Lord, to bring our Mia home."* Bonnie sniffed and wiped away the tears. *"Her family needs her, Lord. They have suffered so much. Please don't take this child from them. From all of us. I know she will serve you and be a blessing to many. In all things, may thy will be done. Amen."*

Now, holding Ginger and staring out the window, a smile slowly lifted the corners of her mouth. "Thank you, Lord," she murmured. The sun shone through the light rain that had been falling since daybreak. And there, in the distant sky, shone the palest rainbow. "Do you see that, little one?" she said to her four-legged best friend. "Yes, I believe God has given us a sign. She's going to be all right."

Bonnie giggled as Ginger tried to cover her with puppy dog kisses.

"I think we should call Val. What do you think?" More kisses and a tail wagging furiously seemed to show agreement... or the need of a treat. So, Bonnie gave her Gingersnap one of her favorite treats, which the dog quickly took to her bed to savor, and grabbed the phone.

When her friend answered, all she could think to say was, "Val, Mia's going to be okay. I'm sure of it."

"Thanks, Bonnie. I appreciate that, but how can we be sure?"

"Let's just call it blessed assurance." Bonnie didn't know if Val was convinced, but she hoped her words may have helped and given her strength.

They went on to discuss plans for their usual Thursday night bridge game, which both agreed should be cancelled—especially since it would have been Sarah's week to host—and Bonnie suggested an alternative project.

"I was thinking maybe Kathy, you, and I could still get together Thursday and prepare a couple more meals for Sarah and the family. I mean, hopefully Mia will be home, safe and sound, by then, but either way—"

"Yes, let's do that," Val interrupted. "And do we have to wait until Thursday? How about if we check with Kathy, and if she's not too busy packing for her move to New York, could we do it tonight?"

"Well, I don't see why not. If you don't mind Joe helping out."

"Oh no, I'm sorry. Do you guys have plans for this evening?"

Bonnie laughed as Ginger jumped into her lap. "Well, to tell the truth, we've been getting together for a visit nearly every day—or evening—for the last few weeks. But one of the things we enjoy doing is cooking together. I'm sure he'd love to help."

***

Bonnie heard Joe's special knock and got to the door almost as fast as Ginger. And as soon as Joe finished his ritual greeting with his furry little friend, he took Bonnie in his arms.

"I missed you," he said giving her a gentle kiss.

"Oh Joe, it hasn't even been twenty-four hours since you left." Bonnie heard herself giggle and realized she sounded a bit like a school girl. And she thought Joe was being awfully silly but loved hearing it. After all, she had to admit she'd been just as anxious to see him again today. "Come, sit down."

"All right, but do you mind if a grab a soda first?"

"Sure, there's root beer in the fridge." Bonnie had started keeping his favorite soft drink stocked in her refrigerator ever since he'd brought his own a few times. When he returned with his can of soda—he never bothered with a glass and ice—Bonnie patted the sofa cushion suggesting he come sit by her side.

Joe scratched Ginger behind one ear, and the little Pomeranian hopped from Bonnie's lap to his. "Did you decide where you'd like to go for dinner tonight?" he asked.

"Well, about that..." Bonnie told him what she had suggested to Val and how she hadn't had the heart to say no when asked if they could do it tonight instead of Thursday. "And I think it would be a good distraction for her. Take her mind off worrying for a couple of hours. Do you mind terribly?"

"Don't be ridiculous. How could I possibly mind?" He reached over and patted her leg. "That's one of the things I love about you, Bonnie. You have a beautiful habit of putting other people's needs ahead of your own."

"Thanks for understanding, Joe. And I hope you'll stay and help. I already told Val you'd probably want to... but obviously you don't have to..."

"Don't be silly. Sure, I want to stay. Just give me an apron and put me to work." Joe took her hand in his. "But can I ask a favor?"

"Why yes, anything."

"Do you mind if I stay for a while after the ladies leave?"

"Of course, dear, I'd like that." Bonnie thought she saw relief on his face.

"Good," he said. "There's something I'd like to discuss with you. Something important."

Bonnie's curiosity was piqued, but they were interrupted by a knock on the door. She would have to wait until later to find out what it was all about. But when she stood to answer the door, Joe quickly got to his feet, took her by the shoulders and planted a quick kiss on her cheek.

"Until later," he said with a twinkle in his eye.

Before long Val, Kathy, Bonnie, and Joe were working on menus for comfort food and scouting for ingredients in Bonnie's pantry to see what they could get started on immediately. All the while Bonnie clung to the memory of God's assurance. *Mia will be coming home.*

CHAPTER THIRTY-SIX – MIA

*H*e's back! Mia jumped off the bed and went to the window. It was so dark. She couldn't see a thing, but she could definitely hear a vehicle coming down the road. Habit made her reach for her phone to check the time. But Benson had taken her phone. *How long did I sleep?* Mia felt fear crawling up her back. It grabbed her by the throat and threatened to strangle her. *Breathe,* said a voice from deep inside.

She looked from left to right, eyes becoming accustomed to the dark, then dashed through the doorway, down the short hall, and into the living area. There was only one way in and out. She had to get out the front door and out of sight before he came around the curve that led to the old bridge.

Mia opened and escaped through the front door, quickly closed it behind her, and flew down the few steps. Looking around, she tried to get her bearings and wondered if she could cross the bridge in time to hide on the other side. No.

He's getting close. I've gotta hide. She saw headlights bounce eerily through the trees then disappear, and clouds slid sleepily in front of the moon, taking away the little light she needed to find her way. Turning sharply to the left, she fell into an old, overgrown holly bush, managed to roll out of it, and rounded the corner of the cabin as she heard tires drawing closer.

She ran toward the back, and the moon peeked out to show her the little bit of open area, overgrown with weeds, and then nothing but woods. Mia was suddenly immobilized by fear. Fear of what lay behind—Benson locking her up again... or worse—and fear of what lay before her.

Mia never thought of herself as a coward, but neither had she ever been alone in the woods at night. Hearing how close Benson must be, she swallowed the knot in her throat and pushed herself into the woods. It didn't take long for her to discover the need to slow down and feel her way. The trees soon hid any sign of moonlight as their thick canopy created a dark cave full of strange sounds. *How far should I go? Oh God, don't let him find me.*

She hoped he wouldn't search the woods, but the sound of the vehicle coming to a stop forced her to go deeper. Hearing footsteps, Mia began to run blindly. She made pretty good progress until her foot caught in the thicket.

Mia went down hard. She gasped and, looking back over her shoulder, scrambled to her feet and took a few more steps. Continuing more cautiously, hands out in front of her, she covered another ten or fifteen yards before hitting her foot and leg on a huge boulder. She leaned against the rock, circled it, and sank to the ground. Feeling battered and broken, Mia prayed her rock would keep her safe from Benson, the crazy kidnapper.

CHAPTER THIRTY-SEVEN – SARAH

Sitting in the back of Agent Carter's unmarked car, Sarah sat wringing her hands until Craig reached over and took one of them in his.

"I know this is the right road now," Holly said from the front passenger seat. "I remember that old chapel with the broken-down barn on the opposite side."

"Let's hope so," said Carter. "As dark as it's getting, we might have to give up until tomorrow if this one doesn't pan out."

Sarah hated even contemplating that possibility. This had to be the right road at last.

They had just left the paved road about a mile back and following this winding dirt trail seemed treacherous to Sarah, especially the way Carter drove. Unsure if it was motion-sickness or fear, Sarah fought the rising nausea. She took a deep breath in through her mouth and blew it out slowly. It didn't help.

Holly looked over her shoulder. "I'm sure this is the right way, Sarah. Hang in there."

Sarah tried to smile her assent but knew her face didn't fully cooperate. She couldn't smile when every nerve in her body quivered with foreboding. This road reminded her of the setting for a horror movie, and she half expected someone wearing a hockey mask and carrying an axe to jump out in front of them at every turn.

"There, you can see the bridge up there in the distance," Holly nearly shouted, sitting forward in her seat. "I remember we crossed that little bridge, came around a curve, and there was the cabin."

Eyes locked on the road ahead, Sarah gasped when it suddenly went dark. "What happened? What's wrong?" she asked pulling herself forward to be sure Carter could hear her.

"Nothing wrong," he answered. "Just don't want to announce that we're here. If this Ben is in there, we don't need him to see us coming. Mrs. Garfield, you said to the best of your knowledge he doesn't own a gun, right?"

Holly assured Carter he hadn't. "I would have feared for my life if he had."

Sarah shivered, remembering the fear she'd read in Holly's eyes when she first entered therapy.

Craig put his arm around Sarah, and she felt the tension in his body. It matched her own. She leaned into him to keep from collapsing. Though she heard Holly's reply that he'd never had a gun when they were together, Sarah knew that didn't mean anything. *Funny,* she thought, *I never considered the possibility of a weapon until Carter mentioned it. But that doesn't mean he doesn't have one now.* The possibility added a new layer to her mounting apprehension.

Apparently, her husband was having a similar reaction. When he withdrew his arm, began staring out the window and wringing his hands, Sarah felt the chill of distance growing between them again.

Carter had slowed down and rolled across the bridge and into the clearing. Sarah wondered how he'd managed to navigate the road in such darkness. Now the cloud that had masked the moon and left the road in near blackness moved on and revealed the outline of a cabin in the gloom.

Sarah turned to her husband. "It's the cabin in Mia's drawing," she said. Even in the dim light she could see Craig's jaw had dropped.

"Yeah," he said. "Jeez."

The cabin was dark. But there was no blue pickup truck parked where it had been in the drawing. Sarah's heart sank.

"Doesn't look like anybody's here," Carter said turning in his seat. He looked through the back window, and Sarah's eyes followed. Webb and Evans had been following in another unmarked car and rolled in behind them. "All right people, just sit tight while we check it out." He climbed out of the car, closing the door quietly, and waited. Sarah saw the two detectives join him, and then they disappeared into the darkness.

No one spoke a word, nor barely breathed, as they waited without knowing what to expect.

Sarah jumped when moments later, appearing out of nowhere, Carter opened the car door. Stretching her neck, she looked for Webb and Evans, but Carter was alone.

"There's no one here."

The agent's words punched her in the stomach and took all of her air. From somewhere far away she heard Craig's voice. He was asking something. Sarah couldn't focus.

Where is she? What has he done to my daughter?

"But I was so sure this was his father's cabin." Holly sounded defeated.

"Yeah, I'm pretty sure you were right about that. They were here," Carter said. "But there's no one here now."

"How do you know they were here?" asked Craig.

"Well, um... there are indications that, uh, someone was kept here against their will."

Sarah finally found her voice. "How? How do you know it was Mia?" She knew it was a stupid question even as she heard the words coming out of her mouth. This was *the* cabin. That monster brought Mia here. *Where is she?*

Craig had gotten out of the car and come around to open her door. Dazed, she took his hand and let him help her out. When her feet touched the soft earth, she remembered all the rain they'd had over the weekend. The smell of damp leaves assaulted her nose. "Where are we going?"

"Didn't you hear him?" Craig tilted his head toward Carter. "He wants us to take a look around and see if we recognize any signs of Mia being here."

Sarah's eyes widened in dismay. Craig caught her as she stumbled over a root in the path near the steps and helped her to the door where they entered and found Webb and Evans examining its contents.

"If you'd just look around, Mr. and Mrs. Reed... I don't think there's anything of your daughter's here, but..."

Sarah didn't hear whatever Carter said after that. She stared in horror at the crate, the cage with an old dirty blanket and pillow. She saw the dirty plate and crumbs in one corner and knew in an instant this had been her child's prison.

"Strange how it's been dragged over by this table," Agent Carter was saying. "You can see by the marks on the floor it had been in that corner at one point."

Sarah stood immobilized lost in a whirlwind of guilt and self-condemnation. *This is my fault. He did this because he hated me.* She wondered how she'd ever explain it all to Mia, and if she'd ever be able to make it up her.

Craig finally put his hand on her back to guide her back out into the night. "Let's go." Uncomprehending, she pulled back looking around frantically. "Didn't you hear Carter, Sarah? He said they're not here and we might as well head back to the station."

Sarah didn't hear any more after that. Something had caught her eye through the blur of new tears. She brushed the tears away to see more clearly and fell to her knees. "Mia," she sobbed, "oh God," she raised her head and looked into the pain in her husband's eyes. "Craig, it's her bracelet. The one Betsy made for her."

That's when they heard the scream.

CHAPTER THIRTY-EIGHT – SUSAN

Susan closed the book and sighed. She'd read this particular one—*Will You Be My Friend*—to Elizabeth so many times, she barely needed to look at the words. Leaning over to kiss the child goodnight, she breathed in the scent of her hair. Though Elizabeth sometimes objected to using "baby" shampoo, Susan hadn't yet made the switch from Johnson's. Some things you just hang on to as long as you can. Especially when you've lost so much time.

"Momma?" Elizabeth opened sleepy eyes to look at her mother and ask, "Is Mia going to be okay?"

"Yes, baby, I'm sure she's going to be home soon, safe and sound." Susan wanted to believe what she said. Mia had to be okay.

"I thought so," the child said. "I think the bad man went away. He doesn't have her anymore."

"What? I mean, what makes you think that, sweetie?"

"I don't know," the little one said before she yawned and slid deeper down in her bed. "I just kinda feel it. Night, Momma. I love you."

"I love you too, sweet girl. Sleep tight."

Susan quietly closed the door behind her, meandered to her own bedroom, and checked her phone to see if she'd missed any messages. No. Her heart sank. *Why hasn't he called?*

Nine o'clock. She opened her contact favorites and looked at the first name on her list. Hubby. Susan had never removed him from the number one spot. *Should I call him?* She quickly tapped the number before she might change her mind.

"Hey, what's up? Is Lizzy okay?" Marty sounded alarmed.

Susan wondered why. Did he only expect her to call if something was wrong?

"No, she's fine. She just went to bed." Susan hesitated. *He's still angry.*

"Oh... well, that's good. So why are you calling?"

"I, I wondered if maybe we could talk."

"Sure," Marty said. "What about? I'm listening."

Susan took a deep breath. This was no time to get angry. "No, not on the phone. I thought maybe we could sit down and talk about us." There was silence on the other end of the phone. "Marty?"

"Yeah, I'm still here," he finally said. "Look, if you've changed your mind about us being together, just say so. I'm a big boy. I can handle it."

"No! That's not what I'm saying. Could you please come over?"

After another long pause, he agreed and said he was on his way. And he was true to his word. Susan thought he must have walked out the door as soon the call ended because he arrived in record time. She had scarcely had time to freshen her makeup and pull a comb through her hair when she saw his headlights pulling into the driveway.

Susan opened the front door before he could knock. "Thanks for coming over. Have a seat. Can I get you something to drink?"

"No thanks," he answered brusquely, sitting on the edge of the far end of the couch, perched like a bird about to take flight. "Susan, I'm here because you asked me, but I'm not riding this rollercoaster anymore."

"But Marty..."

"No, Susan, I mean it. I thought we had it all. Then I got a kick in the stomach and you took it all from me." Susan could see and hear the hurt and frustration. "I thought what we'd had was special, and I thought somehow we had managed to get it back. I believed we could put it all behind us and go back to the way we were." He stood and turned his back to her. "If I was wrong, just tell me, and I'll be gone." Before Susan could answer, he was moving toward the door, and she heard the quiver in his voice as he added, "But don't try to keep me from seeing my Lizzy."

"Marty, don't go." The knot in her throat made it hard to speak, but she managed, "I want you."

Marty spun around. Susan looked at the tilt of his head and his wrinkled brow. He didn't understand.

She patted the sofa cushion, and he took his seat but this time he leaned back against the cushion and faced her. "Susan, you know I want you too, but I can't do this if it's going nowhere."

"Sweetheart, I'm sorry. I'm sorry I hurt you before, and I'm sorry I hurt you again last night... but you misunderstood." Susan slid closer and took his hand in hers. She hoped it wasn't too late. "I don't have any secrets, I swear. It's only that there are things about me—I mean the new me—that you might not know or understand." She took a breath and steadied her voice. How could she explain how much she changed—her philosophy, her strength, her independence—since being in recovery? "You keep saying we'll be like we were, but I'm not the same person. I've changed. Things will be different, and... and maybe you won't..."

"Susan Walters, stop," he said softly. "Don't you think I know you've changed? We've spent enough time together these past months for me to see that. And believe me, there's nothing about the new you that scares me."

Susan couldn't speak. She looked at the man she loved through a blur of tears.

Then the tension was broken when he added with a sly grin, "I rather like this new and improved version."

Susan wasn't sure how they both got to their feet and into each other's arms so quickly, but she knew that's where they belonged, for as long as they both shall live.

CHAPTER THIRTY-NINE – MIA

Mia gasped and clapped a hand over her mouth. She hadn't meant to scream, but as she was peering out from behind her hiding place, something had grabbed her by the hair. When she jumped and screamed, it immediately let go. She jerked around to see what new horror had befallen her but saw nothing. Plastering herself against the rock she listened. With revulsion she heard the flapping—too close—and knew what had assailed her. A bat.

Panic pushed her to her feet. But she didn't know which way to turn. *What's that?* Mia saw a light moving through the trees in what she was fairly sure was the direction of the cabin. The only choice left to her was to run in the opposite direction. But she hadn't gone more than a dozen paces when she tripped over a stump and crashed to the forest floor.

"This way," she heard a man's voice call. "*He's not alone.*"

Fright forced Mia to her feet again. But when she put her weight on her left foot, pain pierced her ankle, and she went down again.

The cracking of twigs revealed they were getting closer. Mia looked around wildly for someplace to hide, then tried to stand and hobble toward a large tree on her right.

Before she could reach it, she was flooded with light. She swung around to face the source and was blinded by the brightness of a flashlight aimed directly at her.

"Here," the man's voice called out. "I found her!"

Mia conceded defeat by dropping to the ground and covering her face with her hands. She wanted to scream for them to leave her alone, but only managed to whimper, "Please don't hurt me."

"It's all right, Mia. It's okay. We're not going to hurt you. We're here to take you home." The voice behind the light spoke gently, but Mia wasn't ready to trust it. She pulled back as the man reached toward her. "My name is Sergeant Evans. Look, here's my badge." It looked real enough. "Your parents are here, too."

Mia's head jerked up. She tried to see beyond the sergeant, but all she saw were two other men. "Are you hurt?" one of them asked.

"No. I mean yes. My ankle... I think I might have sprained my ankle." Squinting and looking beyond the officers, Mia asked, "Where are they? My mom and dad... you said they were here." Allowing Evans to help her up, she tried to take a step. No good.

Evans swooped her up and began carrying her along the path Carter revealed with his flashlight. "They're waiting in the cabin, hon. And boy, will they be glad to see you."

Evans was right about that. As they reached the clearing, Mia saw them. They weren't waiting inside but standing anxiously in front of the cabin. They ran to meet her and the policeman carrying her out, and Craig quickly took his daughter into his arms. Sarah threw her arms around them both as the three cried buckets of relief.

Mia was overwhelmed by everything happening around her... especially the bombardment of questions. Through their tears both parents were asking, "Are you okay?" "Did he hurt you?" "What happened?"

"Do we have to go back in there?" Mia whispered as they approached the cabin.

"No baby, no," Craig said looking at Carter for confirmation.

Carter nodded walking toward them. "No, Mia," the agent said, "but we do need to ask you a few questions if that's okay."

She didn't know how to respond and buried her head on Craig's shoulder. "I just wanna go home, Daddy." She felt the sob shake his body and looked up to see tears filling his eyes. Mia ached with the pain of knowing how much he'd worried... how much her foolish choices had scared him. "I'm so sorry, Daddy." Her words were barely audible.

Craig took a deep breath and slowly pushed the air out through his mouth. "It's all right. It's all right. Don't talk." He stroked her hair, and for the first time since she realized her mistake in trusting Benson, she breathed easy.

Mia felt another hand touch her cheek and met her mother's gaze. "Mom..."

She would have said more, but hearing tires approaching on the dirt road, the words caught in her throat. *He's back.*

Evans rushed to her side. "It's okay, Mia. It's the ambulance we called for you."

"But it's just a sprain. I don't need an ambulance."

It was Carter who explained the protocol—that she would have to go to the hospital to be checked out. Mia clung tighter to her father.

"Can we go with her?" Sarah asked.

"Of course." It was Det. Webb, who had been standing quietly in the background who spoke to the EMT then said, "Mrs. Reed, why don't you ride in the back with your daughter, and the driver said you can ride up front with him, Mr. Reed."

"Just one question before you go, Mia." Carter had taken out his tablet and the headlights provided all the light he needed to take notes. "Did the man who brought you here tell you his name, and did he say when he'd be back?"

"Benson. His name is Benson." Mia choked back the lump in her throat. "And he left last night."

"You've been here alone since last night?" Sarah asked.

Mia nodded. "He was acting different... kind of crazy like. And, and he kept talking about having to get out of here." Mia felt a return of the helpless feeling she'd been fighting. She didn't want to cry again. "I don't think he was coming back." Her words came pouring out faster. "I thought I was going to be left in that cage until..." She couldn't finish the sentence. She couldn't tell them she was afraid she'd die there. She could only give her mother a look that said 'help me'.

Sarah warned Carter that was enough for now, and Craig carried his daughter to the ambulance where the EMTs began their preliminary examination.

Holly, who timidly ventured out of the back seat of Carter's vehicle where she'd remained for so long, approached Sarah. "Is... is she okay?"

Sarah filled her in on the little she'd learned so far and then as Holly apologized again, reminded her she wasn't to blame.

Mia couldn't hear what the two women were saying to each other. When Sarah climbed into the back of the ambulance with her daughter, Mia asked who the other woman was.

"Just a very special friend, Mia. She's the one who helped us find you."

Mia wanted to ask her mother how the lady knew, and she wanted to tell her how frightened she'd been and how she'd finally gotten free. But that would all have to wait as the fatigue of her ordeal caught up with her.

It wouldn't be until Carter questioned her at the hospital that Mia would explain how she'd managed to get to the key and escape her imprisonment.

Chapter Forty – Sarah

Sarah tied the tattered ends of Mia's bracelet gently around her daughter's wrist and watched her sleep, thinking how young and innocent she looked. Though covered with scrapes and bruises and sporting a badly sprained ankle, she had no serious physical injuries. But Sarah knew there could be invisible scars. She prayed the child's innocence hadn't been destroyed by the maniac who'd taken her from her home and family.

A part of Sarah acknowledged that he was a troubled soul, but in this moment, she could not be concerned with him or his problems. She could only thank God for helping them find Mia and pray there would be no long-term ill effects from the nightmare she'd endured.

Holding her child's hand, Sarah looked at the tiny, time-worn bracelet Betsy had given her so long ago. And she remembered how she'd wondered why Mia insisted on wearing it in spite of its sad condition. *I would have had you take it off. Thank God you didn't listen to me.*

Sarah looked out the hospital window to the sky above. "Thank you for bringing her back to us," she said aloud.

"Where's Dad?" The voice sounded so small. So vulnerable.

"He went downstairs to meet your sister and brothers. They couldn't wait 'til you come home in the morning to see you. Your grandparents are bringing them."

Sarah was encouraged by the little smile that brightened her daughter's face. She didn't have time to say more as Mia's three siblings came bounding in ahead of their father. Julie got there first, threw her arms around her sister and started crying while the boys stood at the foot of the bed silently.

When Julie finally let her sister go, Mia glanced at Bobby and locked eyes with Cody. "Well, didn't you even miss me, you two?"

"Nah, not too much," Cody lied, swiping at his eyes.

"Well, I sure missed you guys. Come here!"

"We prayed for you," Cody whispered looking down at the floor.

"Thanks, looks like it worked." Mia smiled past them at her parents.

Sarah, who had been sitting in the only chair in the room, stood and went to stand by her husband. As the children chatted about what they had planned for Mia's homecoming, Sarah rested her head against Craig's shoulder expecting him to pull her close. But not this time. She felt his body stiffen in response to her closeness. Pulling away she wondered if he was still angry.

"Where's Grandma?" Mia called from the bed. "Isn't she here?"

"She sure is, and she and your grandpa can't wait to see you and know that you're all right, but they're downstairs with Destiny." Craig turned toward the door. "I'll go take the baby and send them up."

"I'll come with you," Sarah said. "And you guys take it easy... and be quiet. You can visit for about fifteen more minutes." After a few groans, she assured the children they'd have plenty of time to catch up tomorrow.

"We have our family back," Craig said when they were alone on the elevator. "No thanks to the animal who took her. I hope they catch that S.O.B."

"They will, but let's not think about him right now." Sarah shook her head then unexpectedly giggled.

"What are you laughing at?"

"When I found out how little she'd had to eat since Friday," Sarah shuddered at the thought, "I asked Mia what she wanted most. I figured I'd fix whatever she said when we get her home tomorrow. You'll never guess what she said she's really hungry for... broccoli!"

"Well, I bet we can rustle her up some of that before tomorrow. As a matter of fact, I can run home and do one of those steam-in-bag things you have in the freezer and be back in no time."

"Good idea." Sarah loved his thoughtfulness but wondered if it wasn't—at least in part—simply an excuse not to be alone with her. "And after all she's been through, I think I can do better than that tomorrow." Without warning, her eyes filled with tears yet again. "Thank God we got our Mia back." *But have I lost you?*

CHAPTER FORTY-ONE – VAL

After so many days of off-and-on rain, Val welcomed the sunshine. And it seemed appropriate for the gloomy skies to brighten just as their lives had brightened with Mia's return. She took a sip of her sweet iced tea and looked across the patio table at her husband who was staring out across the yard. He looked totally at peace.

At risk of disturbing his tranquility, Val commented, "It's a beautiful day, Mia's back home where she belongs, all's right with the world."

Andy simply smiled in response.

But Val's mind slipped to how it might have all ended. "When I think what could have happened..." The words caught in her throat.

"Don't," Andy interrupted. "Don't go there. She's safe now."

"I know but—"

"Hey, stop. I know what you're thinking, and it's nothing I haven't played over in my mind too, but Craig says the doctors have checked her out and she's okay. We're lucky."

"No, Andy, not lucky... blessed." And Val meant it. She thanked God for Mia's safe return, and she believed her granddaughter would be okay—physically. But what about psychological damage? Her husband, of all people, should know the emotional damage Ben Garfield may have caused Mia. Many of his clients suffered from PTSD because of childhood trauma they'd endured.

As though he'd read her mind, Andy answered her thoughts. "Val, Mia's mom and her grandfather will both recognize any symptoms of emotional trauma, and we'll get her the help she needs if we see the signs. Come here." Val obediently went to him, and he rose to meet her. "It's over, love." He took her in his arms, and Val felt the comfort and assurance she always found there.

When her husband loosened his hold, Val grudgingly released him and moved her hand to his cheek. Andy responded with a gentle kiss that deepened and made her want more, but she discovered her desires would have to wait.

"Oh, so tempting," Andy said, eyes crinkled with mirth. "But right now, I'd better run into the office and start rescheduling clients." Andy's lips moved from Val's lips to her forehead—from passion to tenderness—before he added, "Are you going to be okay?"

"Of course. I think I'm going to meander down to my rock." She knew he understood since she'd often shared how her special spot brought her a sense of peace. "You won't be gone too long, will you?"

Opening the slider into the kitchen, Andy looked back over his shoulder. "No longer than absolutely necessary. I'll see you soon," he said with a wink.

I'm counting on it.

***

Sitting on the big flat rock, warm from the sun's caress, Val felt the tickle of a ladybug on her arm. "Fly away home," she whispered, and as it did her eyes rose to the heavens. She stared at the brilliant blue sky where the sun slid behind a fleecy white cloud, giving it a halo. Rays of light flowed outward toward earth—toward her—like arms of angels. *Thank you, Lord. Thank you.*

Val sat, giving thanks, aware of nothing but the love with which she felt surrounded, until a sound pulled her from her reverie. Though mildly startled, the crunch of gravel didn't frighten her. She recognized it as footfalls and somehow, intuitively, knew whose steps they were.

"How did you know where to find me, Bonnie?" she asked, turning to smile up at her friend.

"Well your garage was open, your car was in it, and you didn't answer the door," Bonnie said coming to sit by her side on the table rock. "So, where else would you be on such a blessed day?" Bonnie put her arm around Val and added, "I'm so happy and relieved for you all. I just knew Mia would be all right."

"How, Bonnie? How could you be so sure?" Val shook her head and stared down at the water rippling over rocks in the stream. "I wish my faith was as strong as yours. I remember how you taught me to end my prayers with 'Thy will be done,' but I couldn't. Not this time." She looked into her friend's sympathetic eyes. "I was too afraid. What if it hadn't been His will?"

"Oh child," Bonnie said, taking Val's hand in hers. "I'm not a fool. I know talking to God isn't like making a wish or rubbing the genie's lantern. I know we don't always get the answer we're hoping for, and when we don't, it can be very difficult to accept."

In that moment Val remembered how Bonnie had prayed for Frank to live. "I'm sorry. Of course you do."

"And we can't always understand when bad things happen to the people we love, but…" Bonnie said emphasizing the word *but,* "that's where our faith and His love carry us through."

Val nodded and the two friends sat in reflective silence for several minutes.

"So what does a person have to do to get a cup of tea around here?" Bonnie asked.

It wasn't long before the ladies were seated on the patio—Val with another iced tea, Bonnie with a cup of hot—discussing plans for their bridge game the following week.

"I think Sarah will be willing to leave the children by then." Val shared what she perceived to be Sarah's understandable fear of being separated from any of her family right now. "Yeah, by then she'll probably be ready for a little break. This is kind of a family honeymoon time since the reunion." Val chuckled then added, "But they're kids. It won't last."

"Well, it will be good to have our little group together again and get a sense of normalcy and routine back in all of our lives. But not too routine."

Val thought she detected a twinkle in her friend's eyes. "What's that supposed to mean?" she asked.

"Nothing really. You know, we wouldn't want life to get too boring... so I might just give you all a little surprise."

CHAPTER FORTY-TWO – SARAH

Sarah absently tossed her pizza crust on the plate. She never had liked the crust—thought it had no taste—but then even the best part of her slice of mushroom and onion pizza didn't have much taste tonight. She watched her husband and sons wolfing down their pepperoni slices and Julie her second veggie one, but noticed Mia had only eaten half of her first. Earlier in the day, Sarah had prepared meatloaf, succotash, and scalloped potatoes. Mia had dived into that with gusto but been rather quiet ever since.

The entertaining banter between the kids had drifted off with the aroma wafting out of the two big Domino's boxes on the table. Now everyone was immersed in devouring the feast before them... that is, everyone except Destiny—who was busily chomping on her teething cookie—Mia, who was staring into space, and Sarah, who was watching Mia.

As though she had felt her mother's scrutiny, Mia turned and met her gaze. *"I'm okay,"* she mouthed with a smile.

Sarah wanted to believe her oldest child, but she'd been a therapist too long not to understand there might be some residual effects from the ordeal. She vowed to be there for Mia, to watch for any warning signs, and to protect her from any future threat of harm.

When they discussed plans for the following day, Sarah had only grudgingly given in to letting Mia ride the bus to school. At first she had insisted she would drive all the kids to and from school in the future. But when she realized she had a mutiny on her hands, she gave in.

"We have all got to get back to our normal routines, Sarah," Craig said curtly. "Besides, school will be over in a few weeks. Anyway, no sense shutting the barn door after the horse is out."

That last remark had stung. But now, watching Mia, she told herself Craig was right. And Mia would certainly never get in the car with a stranger again. Not for any reason.

So, tomorrow morning Sarah would kiss each of her children goodbye, watch them leave together, and hold Destiny just a little bit tighter before dropping her at Grandma's. She would also hold her breath until they were all safely home again. *And they'll be fine!*

"Who wants the last piece?" Craig lifted it out of the box and searched his sons' faces. They looked at each other for several seconds before Cody said Bobby could have it.

"No, that's okay. You can have it, Cody." Bobby smiled at his slightly older brother.

Craig's eyebrows shot up. "Well, aren't you guys being nice? How about if I cut it in half and you can each have a little slice?"

Everyone seemed to be in a good mood with kindness flourishing. Sarah was certain the abundance of courtesy and consideration would be short-lived and everything would be back to status quo soon enough, but she would enjoy it while it lasted.

"Mom, are you all right?" Mia's voice broke Sarah's reverie and only then did she feel the lump in her throat that she couldn't swallow.

Through a blur of tears, she looked at her daughter, and all the rest of the family who were now looking at her, but she couldn't speak.

It was Mia—not Craig—who came to her side, bent down, and kissed her cheek. "It's okay, Mom. I'm all right... I promise."

"I know, baby. I know." Sarah's breath caught. "I'm just so glad... we're all so glad to have you home."

The room was completely silent for several seconds before Destiny decided to make her presence known.

Bang, bang, bang. Her little hands slapped the tray of the walker she'd been put in to avoid having cookie smeared all over the floor and furniture. Seeing that she had drawn everyone's attention, she squealed with delight. It was the perfect tension reliever. The laughter that followed bounced back and forth between baby and audience.

But when the little one's giggles stopped and she rubbed her eyes, Sarah hastily grabbed a wipe and cleaned cookie from Destiny's face and between tiny fingers. The child's laughter morphed into fussing followed by, "Bah-bah, bah-bah."

"Okay, Dessie," Sarah cooed. "Let's get you changed and get your bah-bah." Sarah didn't really believe in using baby talk, but she loved the way Destiny asked for her bottle and couldn't resist repeating the sounds.

"Can I do it?" Mia asked.

Mia had always been good with the baby—she loved little children—but she rarely offered to change a diaper.

Sarah stood in the doorway watching her oldest daughter as she cared for her youngest. Listening to her playful chatter and Dessie's cooing responses... she felt blessed.

But what if we hadn't found her? Sarah shook off the negative thought and quietly returned to join the rest of the family. However, she found the room which had been bustling with activity moments earlier, now deserted. Checking the kitchen, she found Craig returning from taking the pizza boxes out to the recycle bin.

"Where'd everybody go?" she asked.

"I sent the boys to finish their homework, and Julie went to get her shower awhile." Craig leaned against the counter. "Does Mia really seem okay to you, Sarah? I mean, you're the therapist, and after what she's been through—"

"You mean after what she's been through thanks to me?"

"NO, no, that's not what I said." Craig pushed away from the counter and headed for the door.

"But it's what you implied," Sarah called after him. He whipped back around and came toward her.

Sarah stiffened, unable to read his expression. Before either of them could say anything else a movement behind Craig caught her eye.

"What's going on?"

Seeing the frown on Mia's face, Sarah rushed to her side.

"Nothing. Did you get Destiny settled already?"

"Well, kind of. I mean I got her changed and into her jammies, but I didn't have her bottle."

"Sorry, I was going to get it for you and got distracted," Sarah said with a sidelong glance at her husband. "I'll give it to her if you want to go relax and maybe get ready for bed awhile."

"No, I want to do it, Mom. Besides, looks like you guys are in the middle of something," she added deepening her frown. "I hope it's not 'cuz you're still worried about me."

Craig wrapped his daughter in his arms. "We're not so much worried as concerned, and besides, we're the parents. We're allowed." He ruffled Mia's hair and turned to Sarah. "Right, sweetheart?"

"Right." Sarah smiled to reassure her daughter as well as to hide her confusion. After all their years together, she could usually read her husband like an open book, but tonight she was mystified.

She would have tried to pursue the issue once Mia left the room, but her exit was followed immediately by Bobby flying into the room.

"I don't get this!" He had his math book in one hand and was scratching his head with the other. "It doesn't make any sense," he said, and looked at his father, imploring him for help.

"All right, kiddo. Cool your jets. We'll figure it out." Craig led his youngest son from the room leaving Sarah dumbfounded.

Lord, help me. Help us.

Sarah and Craig didn't have another chance to talk until much later when all five children were finally settled in for the night. But once she was ready for bed herself, Sarah broke the tense silence that had lain between them throughout the rest of the evening. She looked at her husband when he turned off the bathroom light and lingered in the doorway. He appeared to be deep in thought.

"Craig, what are you thinking about?"

His eyebrows shot up, and he looked like he'd forgotten she was in the room. "Oh, sorry. I was just thinking... Mia seems different somehow. I can't quite put my finger on what it is, but..."

"I know," Sarah said looking down at the floor. "He took something from her."

"What d'you mean? She swore he didn't hurt her. I mean he didn't... you know, molest her or anything?"

"I know." Sarah raised her eyes to meet her husband's. "But I think he took her childhood. Her happy-go-lucky spirit." Sarah brushed away the tears that threatened to fall. "She's not the same little girl, and I can sort of understand if you blame me, but—"

"God, no! I don't blame you." Sarah felt herself wrapped in his embrace as he muttered into her hair, "I'm such an ass. I've been so torn up, and... well I think I was trying to deal with my own guilt for not keeping her safe from harm. I guess I took it out on you, but I didn't mean to do that. I shouldn't have." The whole time he spoke he held her tight, swaying from side to side.

"So, we're okay?" Sarah whispered.

"We will always be okay as long as I have you by my side," Craig said putting his hands on her cheeks.

Sarah lifted her chin and felt his lips on hers.

"Are you all right, angel? You're trembling."

"Yes, I am now." Sarah slid her hands behind his head and urged him forward to kiss her again. So lost were they in their embrace, they didn't notice the child at their partially opened bedroom door. Then the door closed without a sound. The only sound in the room was that of two people declaring and showing their love for one another as the two once again became one.

CHAPTER FORTY-THREE – BONNIE

"I'm getting jealous," Bonnie said to Joe. Returning from the bathroom, she stood arms akimbo. "Fine thing. I'm gone for five minutes and come back to find you cuddling another."

"Uh-oh, I think we're in trouble, Ginger." At the sound of her name the little dog tried to cover Joe's face with kisses which made Bonnie's mock indignation crumble into laughter.

She dropped down on the couch next to the smooching pair and tapped her lap. Her furry companion instantly bounded over to kiss her momma. This was one of Ginger's favorite games.

"Ah, my fickle little friend. Now I'm jealous." Joe slid a little closer and casually rested his arm around Bonnie's shoulders. "Okay Gingersnap, I'll have you know you're coming between me and the woman who has stolen my heart."

Bonnie put her hand on Joe's knee. "That's so sweet, Joe." She chuckled. "And there's certainly enough of me to go around." But Joe didn't join in her laughter.

"I'm serious, Bonnie. You know that, don't you?"

Bonnie's smile faded, and a flush crept up her face. "Yes, I think I've known for a while." She slowly raised her eyes to meet his. "And I feel the same."

She saw his face light up and her eyes crinkled. *We're on the same page after all.* Bonnie had worried that perhaps she'd misread his flirtations. Perhaps he wanted nothing more than friendship. *But what exactly does he want?*

"Joe, I'm too old to play silly games so I'm just gonna come right out and ask you." She hesitated for just an instant before pushing out the words. "Where are we going with this?"

"I think what they say these days is, 'We're ready to take it to the next level.' At least I am."

"But what does that mean?"

Joe slid closer and pulled her to him. "May I show you?"

The first time Joe had kissed her, Bonnie had struggled with guilt—like she was cheating on Frank. And though she fought it, she hadn't been able to avoid comparing his kiss, his touch, and everything he did to her husband of so many years, the only other man she'd ever been with, the love of her life.

But she no longer wrestled with feelings of conflict. Bonnie had finally let Frank go. She had given herself permission to love again. It was *time to dance*. And there was no comparison.

Bonnie and Frank had known the passion of youth and carried it with them all the days of their lives together. And when death took her husband from her, Bonnie couldn't imagine ever falling in love again. She knew Frank would always have a big part of her heart.

But now, in Joe's embrace, she was ready to make the plunge. She was ready to give this man the rest of her heart. And his kiss said he was ready, too.

When their lips parted, Joe took her hand in both of his. "I know how much you loved Frank..."

"Hush," Bonnie placed two fingers on his lips to stop him. "This isn't about our first loves—they're gone—but we're here. And I know they'd want us to be happy."

"Well, you make me happy." The corners of Joe's eyes crinkled.

"Ditto." Bonnie took a breath. "And I'm tired of being alone." As if on cue, Ginger scrambled from her little dog bed and jumped back into her master's lap. Bonnie laughed at her little furball and said, "Oh, I didn't mean to hurt your feelings, girl. But a lady also sometimes needs a two-legged companion."

"That's right, Ginger." Joe scratched the little dog behind the ear. "And your momma and I have a whole lot of living to do. And the sooner we get started the better," he said gazing into Bonnie's eyes. His voice and manner grew more serious. "It's become more and more difficult for me to leave at the end of our evenings together. I really don't want to go home to an empty bed. I want to fall asleep with you by my side."

Bonnie wanted the same thing, but until now Joe hadn't said the words that would make that possible. Surely, he knew her well enough to understand she could never lie with him unless their union was blessed by God. *But what if he isn't thinking marriage?* Bonnie held her breath waiting to hear that special question that would change both their lives.

Chapter Forty-four – Val

Val recognized Joe's car in the driveway so she pulled up to the curb. No sense blocking him in since it was bridge night, and he'd probably be leaving soon. She locked the car but took a moment to savor the sound of the evening breeze rustling the leaves before heading up to the house. Val had always treasured that brief period as spring rolled into summer and welcomed the chance to breathe in the scent of freshly mown grass. *God's in His heaven, all's right with the world.*

Feeling like a kid suddenly out on summer vacation, Val kicked off her sandals, picked them up, and shortcut to Bonnie's front door, letting the grass tickle her toes.

She was just slipping them back on when Bonnie threw open the door to greet her. "Come in, come in."

Val's jaw dropped. "Wow, look at you!" Bonnie looked stunning in what Val was sure was a new honey-colored V-neck sheath with lace ruffles cascading down her arms. "Are we playing cards or going to a dance?"

Bonnie laughed and her eyes shone. "No dance, but remember I said I might have a surprise for you tonight?" Val nodded. "Well I do, and it's turned out to be an even bigger surprise than I had planned."

"What is it?"

But before Bonnie could answer, there was another tap on the door, and Sarah poked her head in.

"Can we come in?" she asked, walking through the door with Kathy right behind her. "Whoa? What's up? I'm definitely underdressed for whatever it is."

"Look at you!" Kathy added. "You look gorgeous!"

Val had been looking around and, seeing none of the setup for cards was growing more curious. More suspicious. *What the heck?*

She and Bonnie were close, and Val didn't think they had any secrets, but her best friend was definitely up to something... and she had no idea what that something could be.

She couldn't stand it for one more minute. "Bonnie, what in the world are you up to?"

"It's what we're up to," Joe said coming in from the little study in the back of Bonnie's cottage.

Val wasn't surprised to see Joe. He and Bonnie were often together these days and his car was in the driveway. But she was surprised by his attire.

"We have a little announcement to make, but I'd like to wait a few more minutes."

"Yes, we're expecting someone else to join us," Bonnie said just before a knock on the door signaled a new arrival.

Joe hurried to the door to let them in, and Val's eyes widened at who she saw walking through it. Susan and Marty Walters.

Susan looked around, and when her eyes rested on Val, she smiled sheepishly. Sarah hurried to Susan's side, hugged her, and said how much she appreciated Betsy's help in finding Mia. The two girls were even closer now than they'd been before the kidnapping.

Val and Bonnie's eyes met, and Val knew her friend could see her confusion. But she simply smiled before saying, "So, now that everybody's here—and I know you're wondering why we asked you to come, well, it's because I wanted to tell you, Joe has asked me to marry him..." She turned to look at her fiancé and continued, "And I said yes."

Val joined in the shouts of congratulations but still wondered why Susan and Marty had to join them for that.

"Marty, could you come here, please?" Joe asked.

"And Val, too?" Bonnie said. Holding Val's hand and looking across the room at the others, she said, "As you may or may not have noticed, Joe and I aren't getting any younger, and we saw no need for a long engagement..."

"So, here's the real surprise," Joe said taking Bonnie's free hand. "You're all invited to the wedding. And Marty, I'd like you to be my best man."

"And of course, I want you to be my matron of honor, Val."

"I'm honored, Uncle Joe," Marty said. "But why me?"

"And of course. I'd be honored. When's the big day?" Val asked.

Joe turned away and walked to the study door without answering either question. When he returned, he was not alone. Pastor Barns followed him into the living room.

Jaws were dropping all around the room as Bonnie answered Val's question. "The wedding is now."

***

The ceremony was simple, but included all the important elements for Bonnie and Joe, and following Pastor Barns pronouncing them married and giving the benediction, the celebration began.

Bonnie explained that once they made the decision to get married, both wanted it to be as soon as possible. Planning a large ceremony and getting all their family together—especially with so many living out of state—would take longer than they wanted to wait.

"So, then my lovely bride had this great idea," Joe said still holding her hand. "Why not share the moment with close friends and have a big party with the family later?"

"Yes, and having you here, my dear Thursday night bridge ladies, is wonderful. Joe, do you want to get the champagne?"

Just moments later with everyone holding their champagne flutes, Marty stepped up. "I guess as Best Man I get to make a toast to my uncle and his lovely bride... I guess it's Aunt Bonnie now, huh?"

Everyone laughed but Bonnie insisted, with a wink, that wouldn't be necessary.

Marty spoke of his love for a very special uncle and some of the memories they shared. "I'll never forget you holding our little Lizzy at her christening. There was never any question who would be her godfather. You are one of the best men I know, and you have spent too many years alone. You deserve to be happy. I'm so glad you've found love again and I wish you both many happy years together."

Val noticed Susan wiping away tears and was certain she must be thinking of how close they came to losing Uncle Joe thanks to a hit-and-run driver. And how, in the grips of her alcoholism, she thought she might have been responsible but was relieved to discover she wasn't the person driving. Learning she'd been mugged and her car stolen by the real hit-and-run driver was a tremendous relief, but having no memory of the events of that evening because of her drinking, had been the turning point in her recovery.

Val knew Susan wasn't the same person who had wreaked havoc on so many lives years ago. And she was surprised to realize she was actually happy for her. Plus Betsy would finally have her family together again.

Val was about to step up and make her own toast when Marty said, "Oh and one more thing. Tonight, you asked me to help you out by being your Best Man so I have a question for you, Uncle Joe. Would you mind returning the favor next month when I remarry the love of *my* life?"

Everyone's eyes flew to Susan who had a flush creeping up her cheeks.

When another round of congratulations subsided, Val lifted her glass of bubbly. "Well, thanks to my dear friend's crazy impulsivity," she paused until the titters abated, "I didn't have time to prepare a proper toast, but I can speak from my heart. And my heart says no one deserves to find the joy and happiness of committed love more than you." She looked into Bonnie's glistening eyes and added, "There is so much love inside of you that it overflows and touches everyone around you. Joe, you're a lucky man. I would warn you to be good to my friend, but I can tell by the way you look at her and the love in your eyes, I needn't worry about that. So, here's to the newlyweds... may your lives together be filled with God's blessings."

Val sipped the champagne and let the bubbles tickle her nose. Looking across the room, she noticed Susan's glass had no bubbles. Someone had thought to provide her with a nonalcoholic beverage. Of course, Bonnie always thought of everything.

After the toasts, there were lots of hugs, kisses, and well-wishes followed by Bonnie and Joe moving from person to person, sharing love and laughter. Eventually Val noticed Joe and Marty were deep in conversation, leaving Susan standing alone and looking uncomfortable. On impulse Val approached her.

"Susan, you look amazing, and I just wanted to tell you, I'm truly happy for you and Marty."

Susan's eyes widened slightly before a slow smile lifted the corners of her mouth. "Thank you, Val. That means a lot."

"You're welcome. I'm sure Elizabeth must be thrilled." Those words made Susan's whole face transform. Val noticed how much younger she looked these days, especially when she smiled. "Susan, I just had an idea." Val wasn't sure where the thought came from, but she knew somehow it was right. "Kathy is going to be leaving our bridge group—she confided in us last week she's definitely going to move to New York with her sister—and so we'll be needing a fourth..."

Struck by the realization she hadn't run this by Bonnie or Sarah she hesitated. *No, it's okay.* "So, do you think you might be able to free up your Thursday evenings and join us?"

Val almost laughed at the expression on Susan's face. Her eyes had gone round, and she looked totally befuddled.

"Are you serious? I mean... well, you know... with our history? What I did?"

"Ancient history, Susan." And as she spoke the words, Val knew she genuinely meant it. It was finally time to really let it go. "We were friends once. I'd truly like it if we could be again."

She was entirely taken by surprise when Susan bit her lip then threw her arms around her in a warm hug. Val looked over Susan's shoulder and caught Bonnie watching them. Her look said it all. She approved.

It was a little later that Val finally had a chance to pull her best friend aside. "Bonnie, I haven't seen you look this blissfully happy in a long, long time."

"It's true, Val. Joe has brought joy and contentment back into my life." Bonnie took Val's hands in hers. "It's amazing to think, it wasn't that long ago everything was upside down." Bonnie's eyes roamed around the room. "Nearly everyone in this room was stressed—frightened—but now, Mia's home safe and sound, Susan and Marty have found their way back to each other, and it even looks like you and Susan are okay."

"And you and Joe—what can I say—I sent Andy some texts with pictures, but I can't wait to tell him all about tonight." The words she'd thought earlier in the evening sprang back into her mind. *Truer than ever...*

God's in His heaven... all's right with the world.

Epilogue – Val

"Do you want cheese on your burger, Mom?"

"Absolutely," Val answered, setting the dish of sliced tomatoes and onions on Sarah and Craig's beautiful acacia hardwood table.

The outdoor space behind their lovely home looked so welcoming on this summer afternoon. All the planters were still in full bloom and glistened with droplets from an earlier shower, and the hide-away butterfly leaves of the table weren't hidden but strewn with lots of colorful side dishes to go with the hamburgers, hotdogs, and chicken being cooked by Craig, the grill-master of the day.

Yes, Val thought to herself, *this is a day of celebration, not a day to worry about dieting.* She could still smell the freshness of the early morning rain that had threatened their end of summer cookout. That is, until the smell of grilling meat took over and put her salivary glands into high gear.

Cody's cannonball into the deep end of the pool drew Val's attention, and she stood marveling at how much had changed in all their lives in three short months. Those thoughts were interrupted when Betsy came flying out the French doors, across the patio, and over to the side of the pool. In the few seconds it took the child to get there, Mia swam to meet her and extended both arms in invitation. Betsy, who had been so afraid of the water on her first visit to the pool in early June, now leapt with complete trust into Mia's arms.

"Oh my gosh, Marty, she's in the water already."

Hearing Susan's voice, Val spun around to greet her and her husband. It wasn't so long ago that voice would have set her nerves on edge, but those ill feelings had faded. With time, forgiveness, and prayer, the wounds were miraculously healed, and the one-time friends were indeed friends again.

"I guess we should have put her little swim vest on before we let her out," Marty said.

"Mia's got her." Val gave each of the new arrivals a hug and added the pan of brownies Susan brought to the dessert table Sarah had set up on the side. "And I think you'll be surprised to see how far your daughter has come in the last few weeks."

They watched as Mia pulled the little one through the water having her paddle-kick, then set her on the steps in the shallow end.

"She's so good with Elizabeth, Val... and with the baby too, from what I've seen."

Val had to agree with Susan. "Mia adores Betsy, and she's very responsible for her age. I mean she always has been, but she seems even more mature since... you know, her terrifying ordeal."

"Yeah, how's she doing?" Susan glanced over her shoulder toward the house. "I've been wondering but hated to bring it up with Sarah. I didn't know if it would upset her."

"Not at all," Sarah said. She had just come up behind them and overheard. "She's actually doing remarkably well... And she's finally started drawing again. Just simple things so far, but it's a start."

Val met her daughter-in-law's eyes and the two exchanged a silent message of understanding and gratitude.

"Mia is showing signs of becoming more relaxed," Sarah added, "like she used to be—especially since the news of Ben Garfield's capture."

After he'd been found and arrested in another state, still driving the blue pickup truck, Garfield had made a full, though somewhat incoherent, confession.

Val was one of the few people in whom Sarah had confided, it wasn't until Mia's kidnapper was safely behind bars that she, as a mother and possible victim herself, truly felt safe again. At least safer. Val had worried when Sarah said she might never feel completely secure again, but she saw that the younger woman's eyes no longer darted about each time she left the house as they had in those first weeks after they got Mia back.

Val thought Mia, however, showed no outward signs of fear or anxiety. She only seemed older... more serious...

"The dogs and medium burgers are ready, guys." Craig set the platter on the table near all the condiments. "Chicken and well-done burgers should be good in a few more minutes." He waited until Bonnie, Joe, Susan, Marty, and Val had filled their plates before calling, "Everybody out of the pool! Grub's on!"

Andy, who'd been in with the kids, was the first one out—and Val marveled at how good he still looked in swim trunks—but with hunger winning out, all five children were out of the pool and wrapped in towels in record time.

When Cody and Bobby had hotdogs and chips on their plates they tried to head for the dessert table. "Whoa, guys," Sarah said. "How about some other real food before hitting the desserts?"

They looked longingly toward the brownies, cookies, and watermelon but rolled their eyes and headed back for more "real food."

Julie filled her plate, and Susan helped Betsy with hers, but when Val looked at Mia she saw only side dishes on her plate. "Don't you want a hotdog, sweetie?" Val asked. "Or are you waiting for chicken?"

"No thanks, Grandma. I'm good," Mia smiled sweetly and turned to join her siblings.

Val's furrowed brow was answered when Sarah said, "Don't worry, Mia. We didn't forget you." She had gone in the house and returned with a burger for her and an answer for questioning stares. "Mia has chosen to be a vegetarian now," and motioning Vanna White style, added, "So, voila, a veggie burger for my Mia." The girl's meek smile showed her appreciation.

When the children had all carried their plates to the big blanket spread on the grass at the far end of the pool, Sarah explained this was another change in her daughter. She suddenly couldn't stand the idea of anyone or any living thing being hurt.

"I think we have to respect that," Craig said finally fixing his own plate and joining the others.

"Yes," Andy added, "and I don't know if the no meat thing will last, but I think her heightened awareness of pain and suffering—as devasted as we all are that she had to endure it—will have its positive effects on her ability to show empathy in the future."

Sarah nodded, but when she looked at her mother-in-law, Val knew what she was thinking. Ben Garfield had taken her child, and he took away the innocence of that childhood. Sarah had told her Mia didn't trust people the way she once had. *But her trust in God is stronger.*

Marty turned and said to Susan, "Guess you'd better brace yourself."

"What do you mean?"

"It probably won't be long 'til you have to start cooking meatless meals for Lizzy."

It was Susan's turn to roll her eyes. "Oh great."

Everyone chuckled at the idea, knowing Betsy idolized and wanted to be just like Mia. Marty laughed the hardest, then threw his arm around his wife, and kissed her.

"Oh jeeze, there go the newlyweds gettin' all mushy."

Marty grudgingly let his wife loose. "Okay, Uncle Joe, so now that you and Bonnie have been married all of about three months, you don't play kissy-face anymore?"

"A gentleman doesn't kiss and tell, young man," Joe said feigning indignation.

"He'd better not." Bonnie winked. "But I can... let's just say we may be old, but we ain't dead." Such a comment coming from the most refined among them, brought the house down.

***

It was many hours later that Val and Andy, exhausted from a long day, climbed into their king-sized bed. "Today was really nice, wasn't it?" Val said softly.

"Yeah, it certainly was. You know what else is nice?"

"What?"

"You and me... together."

Val liked the sound of that and had a pretty good idea what was on his mind. "Andrew Reed, are you getting frisky with me?"

"It's like your buddy, Bonnie, said, 'We may be old, but we ain't dead'."

And then, as Andy took her in his arms and their lips met, Val knew she had never felt more alive.

CHAPTER 1

Greta stared at her reflection in the mirror. Wrapped in her own arms, it was the closest thing to a hug she would have on her fifteenth birthday. Sure, there would be cake and candles, and she would blow them out, and then watch as her wish went up in smoke. It was a simple wish, but like every other year, she knew it was foolish to believe it would ever come true.

"Happy birthday to me," she whispered.

Her light brown hair with golden highlights flowed softly, framing her fair skin and blue eyes. She recognized her German ancestry and knew boys were attracted at first glance. Sad eyes returned the stare until she turned away, remembering how Jimmy had smiled and waved after school yesterday... and how she'd pretended not to see him.

Since fifth grade, boys had been vying for her attention. Greta was flattered but knew better than to respond. All through middle school those same boys had teased and pursued her. Sometimes she wondered what it would be like to hang out with them, just to be normal. But now in high school, when Jimmy really did ask her out, she'd pushed him away.

Maybe someday... but not now... unless...

Greta picked up her sketchpad and pencil, sat at her desk, and began drawing. This was her escape, her art, her dream. It was only a temporary one though, as reality crept back into her mind. She wondered what Jimmy must think of her and decided to give it one more try at dinner.

"No! You're a fourteen-year-old child. Absolutely not." Uncle Don didn't even look up from his plate as he loaded his fork with another chunk of meat.

"I'm fifteen... and it's—" Greta began, but was cut off.

"Since when?" he asked, then grunted when his wife whispered, "It's her birthday."

Taylor shot her a warning glance. "Oh, yeah, well you're *still* a child, and the answer is still no," he finished emphatically.

Not so much as a Happy Birthday, Greta thought, pushing the food around her plate. She screwed up her courage to try again. "But, it's not really a date. I mean, it's a group of us that..." The look on her uncle's face choked out the rest of her sentence. Silence.

"Don," Kim Taylor said softly, "maybe since it's her birthday..."

"I said no!" he bellowed. "And if I want your opinion I'll ask for it."

Since going to live with them after her father and grandmother's tragic deaths, Greta had learned her aunt seldom dared to express disagreement with her uncle.

Not another word was uttered. Greta saw her aunt's look of pity and knew it was hopeless. The rest of the meal dragged on in uncomfortable silence.

As Greta brooded, she remembered that her cousin Bobby had been just fifteen when Greta had moved in. "Bobby dated when he was fifteen," she said meekly.

Five years older than her, Uncle Don and Aunt Kim's son Bobby was away at college now. But Greta could remember how he had often stayed out late that first year she'd moved in with them.

"You're a girl. It's different for girls," Uncle Don said. "You know what all boys want from you." He glanced her way and Greta looked back down at her plate. "And I'm going to see they don't get it!"

Greta knew. Yes, of course she knew. Uncle Don had taught her all about that subject.

About the Author

Gloria Bostic is a retired special education teacher from York, Pennsylvania. As a Masters level clinical psychologist, she also worked with women and children to help them overcome abuse. She lives in Dover, PA, with her husband, Lee, and enjoys spending time with her three sons and grandchildren.

Also by Gloria Bostic...

Deception Bridge (Book 1)

Valerie Reed is plagued by migraines, insomnia, and a growing anxiety that her happily-ever-after is about to come crumbling down. Tormented by the fear of losing her husband of nearly thirty years, she hangs onto the one thing she knows she can count on – her friendship with the women in her bridge group.

They provide a safe-haven with warmth, laughter, and trust... until that trust is broken.

As Val searches for a way to save her marriage and learn to trust again, her life and her bridge group go through unanticipated transformations. Their lives will never be the same, and Val wonders if the power of prayer will be enough to save them all.

Broken Contracts (Book 2)

Through faith and forgiveness Valerie and Andy Reed's marriage has survived and grown stronger in spite of Andy's brief affair five years ago. However, the consequences of his tryst with Susan Walters, a former member of Val's bridge group, may now turn their world upside-down once again.

As Susan's marriage falls apart, all she wants is to be a good mother to the child she had always longed for... yet her life is becoming unmanageable as she continually succumbs to the need for her next drink.

When Valerie, Bonnie, Sarah, and Kathy gather around the bridge table, they share more than the game. Only time will tell what's in the cards.

Out of the Storm

Greta Friedman travels from victim to victory in this story of a young woman's search for the life she's been denied. A childhood filled with loss and abuse leaves her desperate to find love and normalcy, but as a young adult Greta is frustrated by unanswered prayers and a pattern of relationships that end badly... until she meets someone special. When Gabe Engel mysteriously comes into her life, Greta begins the journey that will give her the strength to escape impending danger and finally make her dreams a reality.

The Greatest Aunt

It's a scary time for Flora when she learns her parents must go away. She will have to go live with her great-aunt, but can't understand why they call her great. Flora happily discovers why and agrees!

www.ingramcontent.com/pod-product-compliance
Lightning Source LLC
Chambersburg PA
CBHW061134200626
46817CB00016B/1384